KAMALA

FEMINIST FOLKTALES FROM AROUND THE WORLD | Vol. II

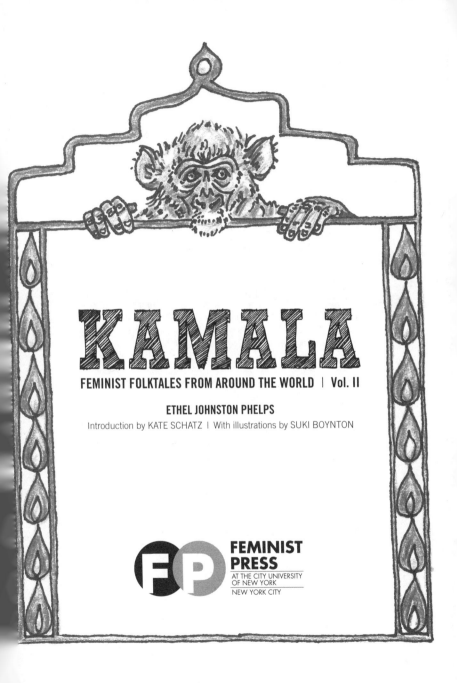

KAMALA

FEMINIST FOLKTALES FROM AROUND THE WORLD | Vol. II

ETHEL JOHNSTON PHELPS

Introduction by KATE SCHATZ | With illustrations by SUKI BOYNTON

FP
FEMINIST PRESS
AT THE CITY UNIVERSITY OF NEW YORK
NEW YORK CITY

Published in 2016 by the Feminist Press
at the City University of New York
The Graduate Center
365 Fifth Avenue, Suite 5406
New York, NY 10016

feministpress.org

First Feminist Press edition 2016

Copyright information continues on page 154

This book was made possible thanks to a grant from New York State
Council on the Arts with the support of Governor Andrew Cuomo
NYSCA and the New York State Legislature.

First printing October 2016

Cover design, text design, and illustrations by Suki Boynton

Library of Congress Cataloging-in-Publication Data is available for this title.

*For Rachael, Jenny,
and Nancy,
who love tales of magic
and adventure*

CONTENTS

INTRODUCTION

KATE SCHATZ

I love this book—but that's no surprise. I'm a feminist author, an amateur historian. A literature lover, an activist mama. I've always loved fairy tales and folktales. I was a women's studies major. *Of course* I love this book!

Point is, I'm an easy audience.

So I put this book to a real test. I announced to my almost-seven-year-old daughter (six and three-quarters—she likes to be precise) that we have new bedtime reading material. And together we read the stories in *Kamala*, night after night. We curled up in her top bunk, her little warm body pressing in close to mine when we met the ogre, stiffening in anticipation when the prince ate the apple, relaxing and laughing in triumph when Kamala tricked the thieves. We giggled at the clueless giant and guffawed at the horse-bride. And in the grand tradition of eager-yet-sleepy children all over the world, each night she begged for *just one more story*. One night I said no, it's late, and turned off the lamp. In the not-quite-dark room, she picked up the book in quiet defiance and read on in the fading light. I let her—how could I not?

What might my daughter dream of after devouring these tales? I wondered. Would she become a talented queen in disguise, on a journey to save her husband? Brave Súmac with her magic fan? A radiant maiden emerging from a lake? With each story, the possibilities expand.

Kamala is the second volume in a series derived from the classic *Tatterhood and Other Tales*, which was originally published by the Feminist Press in 1978. (The new *Tatterhood* was published in 2016, with an introduction by Gayle Forman.) That same year, the Susan B. Anthony dollar was approved for circulation, Buffy Sainte-Marie was on *Sesame Street*, and San Francisco held the first-ever Take Back the Night march. Audre Lorde's *The Black Unicorn*, bell hooks's first book of poetry, and the Combahee River Collective's "A Black Feminist Statement" were all published. Judy Chicago worked to finish *The Dinner Party*. One hundred thousand people marched in Washington, DC, to demand an extension for the ratification of the

ERA. And on an exceptionally hot California September day, I was born, right into the final years of second wave feminism.

In the grand tradition of Joan Didion, I believe that these events are all totally, utterly connected. They are the conditions that produced *Tatterhood* and *Kamala* and they are the conditions that produced me.

During my childhood I read approximately one million books, but somehow I never encountered these stories. I now know, though, that many of my friends did grow up with *Tatterhood and Other Tales*: they recall it as "an absolute favorite" that was "beloved." One friend is currently reading her tattered original copy to her daughter, hoping it doesn't fall apart before they get to the end.

That well-worn copy (and the thousands of others that live in homes around the world) is why the Feminist Press needed to bring these stories back *now*. The four-volume series makes something old new again—which is, after all, what fairy tales have been doing for centuries.

There are reasons that certain stories are told over and over, across generations. We return to these "master narratives," revising them to reflect new times and cultures. Fairy tales imprint messages, mores, and lessons; they explore crucial human experiences: love, loss, battle, the struggle to support a family. They teach us how to treat a friend or a stranger. How to outsmart those who seek to control you. Fairy tales are entertainment and warning, distraction and guide. Illusion and instruction. Their core messages do not stop being relevant—but it matters which stories we tell.

In "Kamala and the Seven Thieves," Kamala is frustrated by her lazy husband, who chooses gossip over work. The story tells us that "being a resourceful woman, Kamala sat down to think of a plan to make the best of their situation." *Boom*. There you go. Rather than sit down and await help like the passive princesses so often depicted, Kamala takes action. The women in these stories are resourceful—and is that not the most ancient of female truths? The importance of being resourceful, of making do, and making good with what you have— when what you have is profoundly limited. When you are denied access to wealth, literacy, property, your own reproductive system—and you still make *something* of yourself and your situation.

More often than not, the women in these stories are providers, via magic, wits, courage, or some combination thereof. When the Lake Maiden emerges from the water, eager to wed the shy shepherd, she brings more than just an enchanted lovely self—she brings a herd of valuable cattle and enough knowledge of healing herbs that she's able to influence generations of physicians. Protagonists like Súmac and the Young Head of the Family save their families, while women like Kamala, Oonagh, and the Lute Playing Queen ultimately (spoiler alert!) save the day and their husbands. Quite often these crafty characters figure out how to work patriarchy, using sexist assumptions that men make about them to their own advantage.

Many of the stories in *Kamala* explore traditional love and romance, with females acting as eager brides—the twist, though, is that the women have agency. In "The Enchanted Buck," Lungile is a young woman whose first marriage prospect was ruined by accusations of witchcraft. After discovering that a "beautiful buck" is actually a powerful chief, the young man tells her: "You will be loved and honored if you will be my bride." It's the next line that gets me: "Lungile consented with great joy." Lungile *consented*. With great joy.

Here is a question that haunts me after reading these tales: Who cast the spell over fairy tales, stealing these fierce, bawdy stories from the mouths of mothers and transforming the strong girls at the center into damsels in distress? Who gathered up these exhilarating myths and then added one thousand cups of sugar, the tears of a lonely princess, and the sweat from the brow of a woodsman? What foul sorcerer removed independence, spice, sass, cunning, and wit? There are answers—Hans, those brothers, Walt, five thousand years of patriarchy—but really, the more important question is: How do we *return* them? *How do we break the spell?*

With books like this, obviously. And when the spells of sexism are broken, women consent with great joy. They choose their lovers, they rescue their fathers, they pass their wisdom down through generations. They bring prosperity, end droughts, and outwit dastardly trolls—and they always get the best of those who try to cross them.

PREFACE
ETHEL JOHNSTON PHELPS

The tales in this book are old stories about magic and adventure. They are stories that ordinary people in the past told to entertain their families and friends. The stories were not originally thought of as "children's tales," but generations of children have loved hearing them.

The people in these tales do not behave the way girls and boys, women and men, have usually been expected to behave in real life and in stories. The heroes are not superior; they are human and vulnerable. The heroines have energy, wit, and sense.

Many of these tales are over a thousand years old, and they have been continually retold—usually by women. Each generation of womenfolk passed on its stories to succeeding generations. In publishing these tales, retold again for today's young people, the Feminist Press is one more link in this chain of women storytellers.

The stories in this book were chosen for a special characteristic that singles them out from other folk and fairy tales.[1] They portray active and courageous girls and women in the leading roles. The protagonists are heroines in the true and original meaning of the word—heroic women distinguished by extraordinary courage and achievements, who hold the center of interest in the tales.

Active heroines are not common among the folktales that survived by finding their way into print, and it is the printed survivals that are the main sources of the tales we know today. Since these tales come from the body of folktale literature that began to be translated into English in the nineteenth century, they reflect a Western European bias. It is therefore not possible to say that the observations made here apply to all folk literature, but only to the published tales we have inherited.

The overwhelming majority of these tales present males as heroes, with girls and women in minor or subservient roles; or they feature young women like Cinderella and Sleeping Beauty, who passively await their fate. Only rarely, scattered among

1. The term *fairy tale* is often used to refer to folktales especially for children; to distinguish folktales dealing with supernatural elements; to signify a tale revised or created by a known author. *Fairy tale* and *folktale* are also used interchangeably. Since all the tales in this book are genuine folktales, I have chosen to use that term.

the surviving tales, do we find stories of girls and women who are truly heroines, who take the leading part and solve the problems posed by the adventure. It must be remembered, of course, that out of the enormous literature of oral folktales, including every culture around the globe and reaching back well over a thousand years, many tales were lost during the centuries of verbal transmission. What proportion of these "lost" tales might have featured active heroines can only be a matter of conjecture.

The awakening nationalism of the nineteenth century brought a sudden surge of interest in the oral tales of the common people. Their tales were seen as a vanishing national heritage that should be collected and preserved. The Grimm brothers began this task with the publication of *Nursery and Household Tales* in 1812; other European and British scholars soon followed.

Only a few women published collections of local tales in the nineteenth century. Almost all the folktale collectors of the period were well-educated males of a different social class from the rural storytellers they solicited. For Europeans collecting in Asia and Africa, the factor of race would be an additional impediment to securing truly representative tales.

Folklorists Andrew Lang, George W. Dasent,

and Stith Thompson, for example, wrote of the difficulties all folklorists experienced in collecting tales. Although women, particularly elderly women, were "the repositories of these national treasures" (a nation's folktales) and the best sources of fairy and supernatural tales, some rural women were reported as unwilling to divulge their store of tales to the collector, for fear of ridicule. These reports referred to various areas of Europe, but the same note is made by Sarah F. Bourhill and Beatrice L. Drake, who published tales gathered in South Africa around the turn of the century. Among black South Africans, they noted, women were most often the village storytellers; however, the women told Bourhill and Drake that they feared ridicule if they told their tales to whites.[2]

Many women did, of course, recite their tales to collectors. But the reticence of some suggests, at the very least, that the tales they were willing to recite were probably those they felt would be socially acceptable and pleasing to the collector. Taking such factors into account, it seems likely that although the preservation and oral transmission of folktales had for centuries been shared by rural women and men, a much smaller proportion of the tales women

2. *Fairy Tales from South Africa*, London, 1908, Introduction, p. v.

knew were collected, recorded, and published. The scarcity of heroic women and girls in the folktales available today may be one consequence.

Nevertheless, women have always been deeply involved in preserving and transmitting this body of marvelously imaginative folk material. They enjoyed and retold the tales while working or at leisure. Their repertory was often large, and they performed with skill as storytellers, passing on the tales to succeeding generations of women. The phrase "old wives' tales," now used derisively, takes on a new and more positive meaning—for the old wives' tales were, indeed, the very rich and varied source of each nation's heritage of folk literature.

A few folktales were published in the eighteenth century specifically for children, but it was not until the latter half of the nineteenth century that the tales definitively became a part of children's literature. Andrew Lang's many volumes of fairy tales attained great popularity. It is worth noting that although Andrew Lang selected the stories, it was Leonora Blanche Alleyne Lang, his wife, who translated, adapted, and retold for young readers the bulk of the collection, which eventually ran to over three hundred stories. Young women relatives and friends contributed the remaining tales. At the end of the preface to each of the books, Andrew Lang made specific acknowledgment of all these contributions. "My part," he wrote, "has been that of Adam . . . in the garden of Eden. Eve worked, Adam superintended. I also superintend. . . . I find out where the stories are and advise."[3] However, Andrew Lang never saw fit to include his wife's name on the title page along with his own.

The Lang fairy tale books, like all collections of this kind, were retold tales, as are the tales in this collection. Adult readers are sometimes troubled by the retelling of folktales, feeling that they should not be "tampered with." But which version of a tale is authentic, and what is meant by "tampering" is not altogether clear.

In fact, the one thing that is certain about traditional folktales is that they have been constantly retold, with new tellers changing details and emphasis to suit both the time and the local audience. Most of the tales exist in many versions or variants, often appearing in different countries, sometimes in different areas of one country. There is no one "authentic" version of a folktale.

While the stories in this collection are retold stories, they are all traditional folktales. In editing and, in some cases, retelling these tales, my gen-

3. Andrew Lang, *The Lilac Fairy Book*, London, 1910, Preface, p. vii.

eral purpose has been to sharpen and illuminate the basic story for the greater enjoyment of children today. Since the evocation of a faraway time and place is a large part of a tale's power to charm, I have kept to the style of the sources and retained much of their language, including old and obsolete words. In some stories, I have changed certain minor external details, but plot and characters are unaltered. Elements of violence or cruelty that serve no purpose intrinsic to the tale, however, have been omitted or moderated; similarly with unnecessary emphasis on remarkable physical beauty. Two of the tales, "Kamala and the Seven Thieves" and "Mastermaid," I have edited down for the sake of a more compact story.

In the distant past, the art of storytelling was a major source of community and family entertainment, and the tales were used and perceived in certain ways not central to present-day needs. Then as now, they offered a temporary escape from reality into the realm of fancy, distracting the mind and stimulating the imagination. Sometimes the tales served to explain or rationalize the terrors of the inexplicable and the unknown physical world. Because their themes echoed the accumulated experiences and beliefs of a people's past, they were capsules of folk wisdom, teaching and redefining moral and social values. Promoting messages by implication, rather than by obvious moralizing, they provided food for thought and discussion.

Encounters with the supernatural usually provide the action in these adventure tales. But whether the plot deals with supernatural creatures or humans, the problems posed test the character of the protagonists. Even though magic or wise advice may help them, it is their heroic qualities of courage or compassion, or their pluck or daring or wit, that enable them to successfully combat the varied forces of "evil." These forces may be greater or lesser, ranging from the cannibalistic giant in "Mastermaid" to the odious squire in "The Squire's Bride." Characteristically, folktales imply that goodness will triumph over "evil."

Although the positive traits displayed by the successful protagonist still have meaning today, it is apparent that the social customs in the old tales, as well as some of their values, are outdated. How is it, then, that they continue to attract and entertain a contemporary audience? One answer is that a good adventure story dealing with the supernatural will always find an audience. The taste for adventures with the irrational and unknown, as well as the need for escape from reality, has not declined, but seems to fulfill a universal need in both adults and children. Some literary qualities of the folktales, too, are timeless—the impudent humor of "The Legend of Knockmany" or "The Squire's Bride," for example. And in the underlying themes of the tales we find a comment on personal and social questions that still concern us: how couples conduct their relationships, how old women face threatening circumstances, how young men and women set about solving dilemmas perplexing to themselves or to the community. Although the themes are played out in a realm of magic spells, giants, fairies, and hobgoblins, the imaginative experience can be the yeast of creative thought that carries over to a more prosaic world. This, too, may be among the reasons that folktales are one of the few forms of children's stories enjoyed by "children of all ages."

Folktales also serve to provide a continuing link with the past, both in the sense of a heritage shared with many, and as a part of the individual's personal past—for it is usually the adult who enjoyed folktales as a child who is eager to pass on to children the same enjoyment.

The emotional satisfaction children derive from the tales arises not only from the protagonist's achievement of success or good fortune against odds, but in seeing justice meted out to evildoers—as it often is to children themselves when they misbehave. Reassured by the traditional happy endings of fairy tales, children can delight in the perilous adventures.

Not all the tales that survive today exemplify the merits just discussed, nor do they meet with the wholehearted approval of parents and teachers. Cruelty and violence in the tales have been a subject of concern for some time. More recently, feminists have criticized the tales for their overemphasis on physical attractiveness, as well as the predominance of female characters who are meek and passive or heartlessly evil.

The danger—or value—of cruelty and violence in children's fiction is, of course, a controversial subject, encompassing television fare and comic books as well as classic literature. Among folktale collectors, the Grimm brothers have been singled out most often for the goriness of their collections. It is useful to remember, however, that folktales were originally shaped for an adult audience, and one that has long since vanished. Many of the descriptive details of folktales reflect the period and the attitudes of the societies from which they sprang. These details are not sacred, nor does their alteration generally affect the basic theme, plot, and characters of the tale. What is important to a tale's meaning is that justice be done unambiguously—a consideration that does not invariably require adopting all of the retributive details of the source. It is not surprising that changed attitudes toward cruel and unusual punishments should influence choices among the tales and the ways in which they are retold, as is the case with the selections in this book.

While feminist critics have raised objections to the convention of the heroine's surpassing beauty, there is no general agreement on this point. Some commentators suggest that the heroine's beauty is not the surface perfection of eyes, complexion, and hair, but the whole beauty of a joyous and radiant person, a symbol of inner beauty, of character and personality. This interpretation of outer beauty, however, is an adult concept that may not be held by the average child; and certainly, for many children, it is discouraging to read that all heroines are extremely beautiful. More important, to be valued primarily for her beauty demeans the other qualities a heroine may possess. Although elements of extraordinary beauty, like those of extraordinary cruelty and violence, are an integral part of some plots, in many tales these are embellishments that can be dropped without affecting the story.

However, while it is possible to revise some elements of folktales without destroying their integrity, the fact remains that the largest number of them portray girls and women unfavorably. We would not want all fictional images of women to be uniformly—and unrealistically—admirable. What is troubling is that although stereotypes of both sexes are common in folktales, there is a marked pervasiveness of older women as frightening hags or evil crones, and of young women and girls as helpless or passive creatures. There are too few surviving tales of likable old women and active, resourceful young women to provide a balanced assortment. In the twelve tales in this book, you will encounter many characters of women and girls, and only one—the malicious sister in "Kupti and Imani"—is a lamentably undesirable character. True, this redresses the balance with sheer force of numbers—but it is a balance that badly needs redressing.

Besides objecting to the folktale conventions mentioned above, some adult readers question the relevance of the omnipresent queens, kings, princes, and princesses to the world of contemporary children. To children, however, as to the country folk who developed the tales, these rulers are symbols of might and wealth. As such, they represent power far beyond a child's command. At the same time, these royal beings move in a fanciful world as easily entered by children as by the rural audience that heard the tales.

For the queens, kings, princes, and princesses of the tales bear little resemblance to any royalty, then or now. Rather, they resemble the well-to-do landowner, farmer, and squire who were in fact the ruling class of the local countryside in Western Europe. Their actions and behavior are those of a prosperous landowner's family. A prince goes to the castle stable to saddle his own horse, a princess hires herself out as a menial servant; a rajah listens to a poor barber's plea and gives him a piece of land—and so on. The "kingdoms" are very small, about the size of a village, and a day's walk often brings the protagonist to another "kingdom." This is a world not only within the grasp of the rural tellers—it is a world that a child's limited experience can comprehend.

The society depicted is usually simple, and in this simple, altogether fictional world, peasants and potentates intermingle and converse, moving apparently with little difficulty from one social level to another. Sometimes high rank or riches are achieved through cleverness, sometimes through an advantageous marriage. Whatever the specific device, it is the virtues and abilities of the protagonist that bring the material rewards so often included in the happy ending.

Marriage is also a traditional happy ending, and one that may appear outmoded measured by the standards of adults who wish to promote respect for the status of single persons of both sexes. Such a progressive view has in fact made headway, supported by the economics of an urban society. The tales, on the other hand, came out of the experience of a rural people concerned with problems of survival and the hopes and fears related to it. Marriage brought the establishment of one's own household and the continuity of offspring, conferring a settled place in the social and economic structure— all of which were necessary for rural survival and prosperity in earlier centuries. Thus, marrying and living happily ever afterward symbolizes all the material, social, and personal rewards achieved by the protagonist, whether male or female; to alter it in such cases would be to rob the tale of its meaning. The marriage ending reflects negatively on women in the general run of folktales only because the "heroine" does little except sit, wish, and wait for this goal, with no power over her fate and no active involvement in choosing or planning the circumstances of her future.

The tales in this book describe many different kinds of heroines and heroes, but all the heroines, in one way or another, take on active roles and make decisions to shape their lives. It is this that sets them apart from the static "heroines" customarily found in folktale collections. Out of the few surviving tales that give us true heroines, we have selected a gallery of strong, delightful women and girls for readers of all ages to enjoy.

KAMALA

FEMINIST FOLKTALES FROM AROUND THE WORLD | Vol. II

In a Punjabi village long ago, there lived a woman named Kamala. Her husband, a barber, was a cheerful fellow who would much rather sit in the dusty square and gossip than practice his trade. So of course they became poorer and poorer, until one day there was not a penny in the house for food.

"Business has been very slow," said the barber. "Even the traders in the market say so."

"That may be," answered Kamala, "but I don't intend to starve. The Rajah is holding a great wedding feast at the palace. You must go to him and ask for something. It would be bad luck to refuse you on such an occasion."

The barber sighed, but off he went to the palace. When he was brought before the Rajah to make his plea, he was too dazzled by the brilliant silks, and the sparkling jewels, and the huge feathered fans moving to and fro, to think very clearly. The thought of food or alms simply flew out of his mind.

"Speak up!" snapped the Wazir.*

The poor barber stammered that he hoped the Rajah "would give him something."

"Something?" said the Rajah impatiently. "What thing?"

"Anything, anything you don't need," blurted the barber.

"Give him a piece of wasteland near his village," ordered the Rajah. This was done, and the barber went home quite relieved that the ordeal was over.

"Wasteland!" exclaimed Kamala, who had had her cooking pots cleaned and ready. "And how will I cook that for our dinner?"

"Land is land," said the barber solemnly.

"So it is—but what good is wasteland unless we till it? Where are we to get bullocks and plow? Or seed?"

The barber could give no answer. So, being a resourceful woman, Kamala sat down to think of a plan to make the best of their situation.

The next day she took her husband with her and set off for the piece of wasteland. Telling her hus-

---

* Wazir is an official title for a high-ranking official.

4

band to imitate her, she began walking about the field peering anxiously at the ground and poking it here and there with a sharp stick. When anyone came that way, they would sit down and pretend to be doing nothing at all.

This strange behavior caught the attention of two thieves passing by. They immediately summoned the rest of the gang and all seven of them hid in the bushes nearby. They watched the couple all day, for they were convinced that something mysterious was going on. After arguing about it endlessly, one of the thieves was sent to find out.

Kamala pretended to be evasive, but finally she said, "It is a family secret. You must promise not to tell a soul." Of course the thief eagerly promised to keep the secret.

"The fact is," said Kamala solemnly, "we've just learned this field of ours has five pots full of gold buried in it. We were just trying to discover the exact spot before beginning to dig tomorrow."

With that, Kamala and her husband returned home, and the thief ran to his companions to tell them of the hidden treasure. The seven thieves set to work at once. All night long they dug and turned over the earth in a perfect frenzy, until the field looked as if it had been plowed seven times over; but not a gold piece—or even a penny—did they find. When dawn came, they went away tired and disgusted, grumbling over their blistered hands.

The next day, when Kamala found the field so well plowed, she was delighted at the success of  her plan. She hurried to the grain dealer's shop and borrowed rice to sow in the field, promising to pay it back with interest at harvest time. And so she did, for never was there such a fine crop! Kamala paid her debts, kept some rice for the house, and sold the rest for enough gold pieces to fill a large earthen crock.

When the thieves saw this, they were very angry indeed. They hastened to the barber's hut and confronted Kamala.

"Give us a share of the harvest money," they demanded brazenly. "We dug up the ground for you. You can't deny that." Kamala simply laughed at them. "I told you there was gold in the ground! You tried to find it to steal it, didn't you? But I knew how to get gold from the earth, and you rascals shan't have a penny of it!"

"If you won't give us a share of it, we'll take it!"

"You'll have to find it first!" Kamala retorted and slammed the door on them.

Nonetheless, she kept a sharp lookout, and that evening she noticed one of the thieves had crept up to the house and hidden himself under the open window.

"What have you done with the gold, my dear?" asked the barber. "I hope you haven't put it under our pillows!"

"Don't be alarmed," she said in a loud voice, "the gold is not in the house. I have hung it in the branches of the nim tree outside. No one will think of looking for it there."

The thief outside the window heard this, as he was meant to, and he hurried off chuckling to tell his companions. When everyone had gone to sleep, the band of thieves gathered under the tree.

"There it is!" cried the captain of the band, peering up into the branches. "One of you go up and bring it down." Now what he saw was really a hornets' nest full of great brown-and-yellow hornets, but in the faint moonlight it looked like a bag of gold.

So one of the thieves climbed up the tree. But when he came close and was just reaching up to take hold of it, a hornet flew out and stung him on the thigh, causing him to clap his hand to the spot.

The watchers below cried out angrily, "He's

taking gold pieces for himself! He's put one in his pocket!"

"I am not," retorted the thief. "Something bit me!" But just at that moment another hornet stung him on the breast, and he smacked his hand there.

"We saw you!" cried the thieves below, and they sent up another man to bring down the gold. But he fared no better for the hornets were now thoroughly aroused, and he, too, began to smack his hands about him. The other thieves danced with rage, convinced he was also pocketing gold pieces.

"They're stealing our gold!" bawled the thieves below, and one after another they climbed up into the tree, eager to get their share of the loot. As soon as they reached the branch nearest the hornets' nest, they all began slapping their clothes as if they were filling their pockets.

The angry leader of the band climbed up last. Determined to have the prize, he seized hold of the hornets' nest. At that moment the branch they were all standing on broke, and they all came tumbling to the ground with the hornets' nest on top of them. What a stampede there was! They scrambled off in all directions with the buzzing hornets in pursuit.

After that Kamala and her husband saw nothing of the thieves for quite a while. They were all laid up with injuries, and the couple was very pleased to be rid of them.

"They don't dare to come back!" said Kamala to her husband. But she was wrong. The gang of thieves was planning its revenge.

One night when it was very hot, the barber and his wife put their beds outside to sleep. The thieves, seizing their chance, lifted up Kamala's bed and carried her off fast asleep. She woke to find herself borne along on the heads of four of the thieves, while the other three ran along beside. She gave herself up for lost; there did not seem any way to escape.

Then the robbers paused for breath under a large tree.

Quick as a wink she seized hold of a branch and swung herself into the tree, leaving the quilt on the bed just as if she were still in it.

"Let us rest here awhile," said the men carrying the bed. "There's plenty of time, and we're tired. She's dreadfully heavy!" And they set their burden down to one side.

Kamala kept very still, for it was a bright moonlit night. The thieves argued over who should first stand guard while the others slept. It fell to the leader, so he walked up and down as guard. Meanwhile, Kamala sat perched up in the tree like a great bird.

Suddenly she had an idea, and drawing the thin white material of her garment over her face, she began to sing softly.

When the leader looked up and saw the veiled figure of a woman in the tree, he was, of course, surprised. But being a young fellow and quite vain about his looks, he at once decided it must be a fairy or peri who had fallen in love with his handsome face. He had heard of such happenings, especially on moonlit nights. So he twirled his moustaches and strutted about, waiting for her to speak.

But when she went on singing and took no notice of him, he stopped and called out, "Come down, my beauty! I won't hurt you!"

Still she went on singing. So he climbed into the tree, smoothing his hair and patting his moustache as he went. When he came quite close, she turned her head away and uttered a long mournful sigh.

"What is the matter, my little one?" he asked tenderly. "You are a fairy and you have fallen in love with me, but why should you sigh so sadly?"

"Aaah," sighed Kamala again. "I believe you are fickle! You will soon forget me!"

"Never!" cried the leader of the thieves.

"Take a bite of this fairy fruit, and then I shall know if you are sincere." As she said this, she plucked a large pomegranate from the tree and rammed it into the thief's open mouth.

Startled, the thief tumbled off the branch and crashed to the ground where he sat with his legs wide apart, looking as if he'd fallen from the sky.

"What is the matter?" cried his comrades awakened by the noise.

"Ah—aagh—aagh" was all he could say as he pointed up into the tree, for his mouth was firmly gagged with the fruit, and he was too stunned to know what had happened.

"The man is bewitched," cried one. "There must be a ghost in the tree!"

Just then Kamala began flapping her veil and howling eerily. *Whoooeeewhooooeeee!* The thieves were terrified. They ran off as fast as they could, dragging their leader behind them.

When they were over the hill and out of sight, Kamala came down from the tree, balanced her cot on top of her head, and walked home.

And that was the end of the thieves' attempt to steal the gold—for the robbers didn't stop running until they reached the next village, and they never came back.

Tales from the Punjab area of India are known for their humor. This is a retelling of **FLORA ANNIE STEEL**'s *"The Barber's Clever Wife," from* Tales of the Punjab *(1917).*

The
Young Head
of the
Family

Long ago in China there lived an old farmer with three sons. Two of the sons who had recently married brought their wives home and all lived together as a family. Since there was no mother in the household, every time the young wives wanted to visit their parents and relatives in another village, they had to ask their husbands' father if they might go, for this was the custom at that time.

They asked to visit their relatives so often that the old farmer became very annoyed.

"You are always asking me to let you go off to visit your relatives," he said. "When I refuse you think me very hardhearted. Very well, you may go, but only on the condition that you each bring me back what I ask."

"Yes, of course," they said quickly.

"One of you must bring me fire wrapped in paper, and the other must bring me wind in paper. If you cannot do that, do not come back!"

The young wives agreed without thinking and happily set out to walk the long distance to their own village.

On the way one of the wives' sandal straps broke, and they sat down by the roadside to fix it. Only then did they realize that it would be impossible to bring back wind in paper or fire wrapped in paper. They sat by the roadside in despair, for they did not want to leave their husbands.

Along came a girl riding a water buffalo. Seeing their unhappy faces, she asked if she could help them.

"No one can help us!" they cried. "What our husbands' father asks is impossible!"

But the girl insisted that she might be able to help, and at last they told her their story.

"Come home with me, and I will show you how to bring him what he asks," said the girl.

Off they went with her to her home, where she showed them a paper lantern with a candle inside.

"There, you see, is fire in paper, and here," she said picking up a paper fan and waving it, "is wind in paper."

The young women thanked her and went happily on their way. After a cheerful visit with relatives and friends in their villages, they took a paper lantern and a fan and returned to their husbands.

"I told you not to return unless you brought the two things I asked for," said the old farmer sharply.

"But we have them," they answered. And they gave him the paper lantern and the fan.

The old man was astonished. "Tell me how you solved this riddle!" he demanded.

Then they told him of meeting the young girl on the water buffalo, and the advice she had given them.

"That is a very clever young woman," the old farmer thought. "She would make a good wife for my youngest son."

So he at once set about finding out if the young girl was already betrothed. Upon learning that she was not, he sent a matchmaker to her family to arrange the marriage.

All the arrangements took place as planned, and after the marriage celebration was over, the old farmer said to his family, "Since the wife of my youngest son is so wise, she will now be the head of the family. You must ask her advice and direction in all things."

The new, young head of the household told the men of the family they must neither go to the fields, nor return home, empty-handed. Each day they were to bring fertilizer of some kind from the farm buildings to the fields, and each day gather sticks of firewood on their return.

In this way their crops thrived, and the family always had a supply of firewood. When there were only a few sticks to gather, they were told to bring back stones. Soon, near the house, there was a pile of stones that could be used for building.

One day a gem dealer came riding by and stopped to examine the pile of stones. Among them he saw a stone that contained a block of precious jade.

He at once went to the house and asked to talk to the head of the family. He was, of course, surprised to see so young a woman, but so skillfully did she manage the bargaining that he finally agreed to pay a very high price for the pile of stones. He said nothing about the jade among the stones, but he promised to return in three days' time with the money.

That night the young wife thought about the

matter and decided the heap of stones must contain some kind of valuable gem.

She went to her father-in-law and told him to invite the dealer to dinner. Then she advised the men of the family to talk about precious stones and how they could be recognized when found on the ground.

While the men feasted and talked, the young head of the family listened behind a curtain. When she had the information she needed, she went outside to the pile of stones and found the one that was valuable. Then she brought it into the house and put it away.

The next day the dealer returned and discovered the valuable jade was no longer there. He realized his trick had been discovered, and he sought out the young head of the family. Again she bargained firmly with the dealer. She would not agree to sell the jade unless he also bought the pile of building stones, and after a long discussion, she secured a proper payment for both.

The old farmer and his family were very proud of her business ability. They were now prosperous and decided to build a much larger, more comfortable new home. Inscribed on the gateway to the new house were the words "No Sorrow."

Not long afterward a mandarin* came by and, seeing the unusual words over the entrance, ordered his servants to set down his sedan chair.

"That is a very arrogant motto," said he with displeasure. "No family is without sorrow! You mock the gods, and I shall fine you for this impudence."

"This family has been fortunate and happy," the young head of the household answered politely. "The words 'no sorrow' mean let all who enter here leave sorrow at the gate."

The mandarin was not appeased. "I order you to weave me a piece of cloth as long as this road!"

"Very well," she answered. "As soon as Your Excellency has found the two ends of the road and told me the exact number of feet in its length, I will at once begin weaving."

The mandarin knew he had been at fault in hastily imposing such a fine, but he was irritated at the young woman's clever answer. He added angrily, "And I also fine you as much oil as there is water in the sea."

"Certainly," she answered. "As soon as you have measured the sea and sent me the correct number

*A mandarin is a Chinese government official.

of gallons, I will begin to press out the oil from my beans."

"Since you are so clever and witty, perhaps you can read my mind!" he snapped. "If you can, I withdraw the fines. I hold this pet bird in my hand. Now tell me whether I mean to squeeze it to death or to let it fly in the air."

"Well," said the young woman. "I am an obscure commoner, and you are a famous official. If you are no more knowing than I, you have no right to fine me at all. Now, I stand with one foot on the one side of my threshold and the other foot on the other side. Tell me whether I mean to go in or come out. If you cannot guess my mind, you should not require me to guess yours."

Of course, the mandarin could not guess her intention and was forced to admit to himself the wisdom of her words. He haughtily took his departure, and the family lived happily ever after under its chosen head.

KATE DOUGLAS WIGGIN *retold this Chinese tale in* Tales of Laughter: A Third Fairy Book *(1908). It is a Chinese version of the clever woman who solves riddles, retold once more by the editor.*

The Legend of
KNOCKMANY

Long ago, in Ireland, there lived a giant named Cucullin. No other giant of the time was his equal in size or strength, not even the famed Fin M'Coul. 'Twas said no other giant had a chance with Cucullin in a fight. So powerfully strong was he that, when angry, he could stamp his foot and shake the whole countryside around him. With one blow of his fist he had flattened a thunderbolt in the shape of a pancake and kept it in his pocket to frighten his enemies. Truth to tell, he liked being the most feared giant in Ireland. He had beaten up every other giant in the land—every one, that is, save Fin M'Coul. As for Fin, Cucullin swore he would never rest until he had caught up with him and knocked him senseless.

Now Fin was not nearly as big a giant as Cucullin, but he was brash and cocky, and he had given out that he'd wipe the ground with Cucullin if ever he had the luck to meet up with him. But Fin, who was no fool, took care to stay well clear of Cucullin.

So matters stood one fine spring day when Fin and his men were up north working on the Giant's Causeway to Scotland. When news came to Fin that Cucullin was headed that way to have a trial of strength with him, Fin was seized with a sudden desire to visit his wife Oonagh. So he pulled up a fir tree, lopped off the branches to make a walking stick of it, and set off at once for his home at Knockmany.

In truth, people wondered why he had built his house at the top of Knockmany, where the winds blew fiercely from every direction and there was not a drop of water. Oonagh had to go down to a spring at the foot of the steep hill and then carry her full pails up to the top again.

"There's a fine prospect in every direction," was Fin's answer. "And as for the water, I plan to sink a well up on top one of these days when I get around to it." He'd been saying this for many years, but of course the real reason for living on top of Knockmany was so that he could keep a sharp lookout for Cucullin or any other enemy headed his way.

"God save all here!" said Fin as he put his face in the door.

"Welcome home, you darlin'," cried Oonagh.

Fin then gave her such a warm smack on the lips that the waters in the lake across the valley curled and bounced.

Fin spent two or three happy days with Oonagh feeling very comfortable, except for the dread he had of Cucullin. But Oonagh soon sensed that something was troubling him.

"What is it with you now?" she asked.

"It's that beast Cucullin," brooded Fin, and he popped his thumb into his mouth. Now Fin's thumb had a magical property. When he put it into his mouth and touched a special tooth, it could tell him what was going to happen.

"He's coming this way," said Fin looking as miserable as a wet sock, "and what to do I don't know. If I run away, I will be disgraced and a laughing stock to all the other giants. Sooner or later I must meet him, my thumb tells me so. But how to fight with a giant that makes a pancake out of a thunderbolt and shakes the whole country with a stamp of his foot? He'll make mincemeat out of me, he will!"

"When will he be here?" asked Oonagh.

"Tomorrow, about two o'clock," groaned Fin.

"Don't fret yourself," she answered. "Depend on me, and we'll settle this once and for all. I'll bring you out of this scrape better than you could yourself, by your rule of thumb."

Fin became very melancholy. Strong and brave

though he was, what chance would he have against that ugly customer Cucullin? "What can you do for me, Oonagh, with all your invention? Sure I'll be skinned like a rabbit before your eyes. I'll be disgraced in the sight of my tribe, and me the best man among them!"

"Be easy now, Fin," she said. "Thunderbolt pancakes he fancies, does he? You just leave him to me and do as I bid."

This relieved Fin very much, for he had great confidence in his wife who had gotten him out of many a pickle before this. Oonagh went to the skeins of wool hanging outside to dry and drew nine long strands of different colors. She then plaited the wool into three plaits with three colors in each, putting one around her right arm, one around her right ankle, and the third around her chest over her heart. Now she knew she would not fail in anything she undertook.

Next she went round to her neighbors and borrowed twenty-one iron griddles, thin, round, and flat they were. Then she kneaded dough for bread and hid the griddles inside the twenty-one loaves of bread she was shaping. In addition, she made one round loaf in the regular way, without a griddle hidden inside. While they were baking, she made a large pot of milk cheese. She then made a high smoking fire on the top of the hill, after which she put her fingers in her mouth and gave three whistles. This was the way that the Irish long ago gave a sign to all strangers and travelers to let them know they were welcome.

Having done all this, she sat down that evening, quite contented, and asked Fin to tell her more about Cucullin. One of the things he told her was that Cucullin's middle finger on his right hand was the magical source of his great strength. Should he lose that, he had no more power than a common man, for all his large bulk.

The next day Cucullin was seen striding across the valley, taller than a round tower. Oonagh took out the old cradle and made Fin lie down in it. Then she handed him a white cotton bonnet to tie over his head.

"Curl yourself up and pretend to be your own child," said she, covering him with a quilt. "Say nothing now but be guided by me."

A thunderous knock on the door shook the house. Fin huddled in the cradle and turned pale.

"Come in and welcome," cried Oonagh. Cucullin bent down to enter, for he was a taller giant than old Fin.

"Is this where the famous Fin M'Coul lives?"

"It is," said Oonagh. "Won't you be sitting down?"

"Thank you kindly, I will," said Cucullin. "Is he at home now?"

"Why no," said Oonagh, "he left the house this morning in a perfect fury! Someone told him a big, bragging, gossoon of a giant called Cucullin was looking for him up at the Causeway, and he set off to try to catch him. I hope for the poor giant's sake Fin doesn't catch him, for he'll make a paste of him if he does!"

"Well," said the huge giant, "I am Cucullin, and I've been seeking him these twelve months. I'll not stop till I get my hands on him."

Oonagh gave a loud laugh of contempt. "Poor fellow! I'm thinking you've never seen the great Fin M'Coul."

"How could I," said he, "with him dodging about and keeping clear of me?"

"It'll be a bleak day for you if you meet up with Fin," Oonagh replied. "But stay and rest awhile, and we'll hope the wild temper on him will cool down a bit. In the meantime I'll ask a civil favor of you. The wind is blowing in the door from the east. If you'd be kind enough to turn the house around? For that is what Fin does when he's here."

Cucullin stared at her in astonishment. However, he got up and went outside with Oonagh, and after pulling the middle finger of his right hand three times, he lifted the house and turned it around as she wished. In the cradle, Fin felt the sweat start out on him, for, of course, this was something he had never done.

Oonagh nodded in satisfaction. "I've always preferred the house this way. Now, since you're out here maybe you'd do one more thing to oblige me?"

"And what's that?" asked Cucullin uneasily.

"After this long spell of dry weather, we're badly off for want of water," replied Oonagh. "Fin says there's a fine spring well under the rocks here. It was his intention to pull them asunder today, but he left in such a rage to find you he didn't have time to do it." And she showed him a crevice in the rocky surface behind the house.

Cucullin looked at it and glowered. It was plain he didn't fancy the job. But he cracked his middle finger nine times and, bending down, he tore a cleft in the rock forty feet deep. Up gushed the spring Oonagh had been needing these many years.

"Thank you kindly," said she, "and now you must come in to share the food I'd prepared for Fin. For even though you're enemies, he'd expect me to make you welcome and share our humble fare."

31

She brought him in and placed before him a half dozen of the specially prepared round bread loaves, together with a can or two of butter and cheese.

Cucullin put one of the loaves in his mouth and let out a thundering yell.

"What's the matter?" asked Oonagh coolly.

"Matter!" he shouted. "Here are two of my teeth out! What kind of bread is this you've given me?"

"Why," said she, "that's Fin's bread—the only bread he ever eats when he's at home. Nobody else can eat it but himself and his little  son in the cradle there. But since you think yourself the equal of Fin, try another loaf. It may not be as hard."

By this time Cucullin was very hungry, so he made a fresh start at the second loaf. This time he gave out a cry louder than the first, for he'd bitten into the loaf harder, not wishing to appear a weakling.

"Thunder and gibbets!" he roared. "Take your bread away or I'll not have a tooth in my head. There's two more teeth out!"

"If you're not able to eat the bread, say so quietly or you'll wake the child in the cradle. There now, he's awake on me!"

Fin gave a skirl that startled the giant, coming from what he thought was a baby. "Mother," cried Fin, "I'm hungry!" Oonagh brought him the bread loaf that had no griddle in it and put it into his hand. Fin chewed it up and swallowed it.

Cucullin was thunderstruck. He thanked his stars he'd had the good fortune to miss finding Fin at home. "I'd have no chance with him," he thought, "for even his little son can easily chew the bread that breaks my teeth!"

"Is it special teeth they have in Fin's family?" he asked aloud as he got up to leave. He had decided he'd rather not have anything to do with Fin M'Coul.

"Why don't you feel for yourself?" answered Oonagh. "I'll get the babe to open his mouth. It's rather far back they are, so put your longest finger in."

Cucullin was surprised to find such a powerful set of grinders in one so young. And even more astounded to find he'd lost the very finger on which his strength depended. With a good hard bite, Fin had taken off his enemy's finger. Cucullin now was powerless.

Fin jumped out of the cradle, and Cucullin, with a shriek of terror, turned to run for it. All the way down the hill he ran, with Fin after him. Fin didn't catch him, for Cucullin could still run fast, even if his magical power was gone. So Fin returned up the hill to find Oonagh cutting the iron griddles out of the loaves. He gave her a hug and a smack, and they settled down to dinner in peace.

WILLIAM CARLETON *published this tale in the early nineteenth century in his collection of stories from Irish peasants.* **W. B. YEATS** *reprinted it in his folktale collection, and* **J. JACOBS** *retold it. This version by the editor is based on Jacobs's retelling, although the original tale probably dates from the sixteenth century when comic parodies of the ancient heroic legends developed.*

Once there was a king who had two daughters and their names were Kupti and Imani. He loved them both very much and spent hours talking to them.

One day he said to Kupti, the elder, "Are you satisfied to leave your life and fortune in my hands?"

"Verily, yes," answered the princess, surprised at the question. "In whose hands should I leave them, if not in yours?"

But when he asked his daughter Imani the same question, she replied, "No, indeed! If I had the chance, I would make my own fortune."

At this answer the king was very displeased, and said, "You are too young to know the meaning of your words. But, be it so, my daughter, I will give you the chance of gratifying your wish."

Then he sent for an old lame beggar man who lived in a tumbledown hut on the outskirts of the city, and when he had presented himself, the king said, "No doubt, as you are very old and nearly crippled, you would be glad to have some young person live with you and serve you; so I will send you my younger daughter. She wants to earn her living and she can do so with you."

Of course the old beggar had not a word to say; or if he had, he was really too astonished and troubled to say it. But the young princess went off with him smiling, and tripped along quite gaily, while he hobbled home with her in perplexed silence.

They reached the hut, and the old man began to think what he could arrange for the princess's comfort. But after all he was a beggar, and his house was bare except for one bedstead, two old cooking pots, and an earthen jar for water, and one cannot get much comfort out of such things.

However, the princess soon ended his perplexity by asking, "Have you any money?"

"I have a penny somewhere," replied the old man.

"Very well," rejoined the princess, "give me the penny and go out and borrow me a spinning wheel and a loom."

After much seeking the beggar found the penny and started on his errand, while the princess went shopping. First she bought a farthing's worth of oil, and then she bought three farthings' worth of flax. When she returned with her purchases, she set the old man on the bedstead and rubbed his crippled leg with the oil for an hour.

Then she sat down to the spinning wheel and spun and spun all night long while the old man slept. In the morning, she had spun the finest thread that was ever seen. Next she went to the loom and wove and wove until, by the evening, she had woven a beautiful silver cloth.

"Now," she said to him, "go into the marketplace and sell my cloth while I rest."

"And what am I to ask for it?" said the old man.

"Two gold pieces," replied the princess.

So the beggar hobbled away and stood in the marketplace to sell the cloth. Presently the elder princess drove by, and when she saw the cloth, she stopped and asked the price, for it was better work than she or any of her women could weave.

"Two gold pieces," he said. And the princess gladly paid them, after which the old man hobbled home with the money.

As she had done before, so Imani did again day after day. Always she spent a penny upon oil and flax, always she tended the old man's lame leg, and spun and wove the most beautiful cloths and sold them at high prices. Gradually the city became famous for her beautiful goods, the old man's lame leg became straighter and stronger, and the hole under the floor of the hut where they kept their money became fuller and fuller of gold pieces.

At last, one day, the princess said, "I really think we have enough to live in greater comfort." She sent for builders, and they built a beautiful house for her and the old beggar man, and in all the city there was none finer except the king's palace. Presently this reached the ears of the king, and when he inquired whose it was, they told him that it belonged to his daughter.

"Well," exclaimed the king, "she said that she would make her own fortune, and somehow or other she seems to have done it!"

A little while after this, business took the king to another country, and before he went he asked his elder daughter what she would like him to bring her back as a gift.

"A necklace of rubies," answered she. And then the king thought he would like to ask Imani too; so he sent a messenger to find out what sort of present she wanted. The man happened to arrive just as she was trying to disentangle a knot in her loom, and bowing low before her, he said, "The king sends me to inquire what you wish him to bring you as a present from the country of Dûr?"

But Imani, who was only considering how she could best untie the knot without breaking the thread, replied, "Patience," meaning that the messenger should wait till she was able to attend to him. But the messenger went off with this as an answer and told the king that the only thing Princess Imani wanted was patience.

"Oh!" said the king. "I don't know whether that's a thing to be bought at Dûr. I never had it myself, but if it is to be found I will buy it for her."

Next day the king departed on his journey, and when his business at Dûr was completed, he bought for Kupti a beautiful ruby necklace.

Then he said to a servant, "The Princess Imani wants some patience. I did not know there was such a thing, but you must go to the market and inquire, and if any is to be sold, get it and bring it to me."

The servant saluted and left the king's presence. He walked about the market for some time crying, "Has anyone patience to sell? Patience to sell?" And some of the people mocked; and some, who had no patience, told him to go away and not be a fool; and some said, "The fellow's mad! As though one could buy or sell patience!"

At length it came to the ears of the King of Dûr that a madman was in the market trying to buy patience. The king laughed and said, "I should like to see that fellow. Bring him here!"

And immediately his attendants went to seek the man and brought him to the king, who asked, "What is this you want?" And the man replied, "Sire, I am bidden to ask for patience."

"Oh," said the king, "you must have a strange master! What does he want with it?"

"My master wants it as a present for his daughter Imani," replied the servant.

"Well," said the king, "I know of some patience which the young lady might have if she cares for it, but it is not to be bought."

Now the king's name was Subbar Khan, and Subbar means patience, but the messenger did not know that or understand that he was making a joke. However, he declared that Princess Imani was not only young and lovely, but also the cleverest, most industrious, and kindest-hearted of princesses.

And he would have gone on explaining her virtues had not the king laughingly put up his hand and stopped him, saying, "Well, well, wait a minute, and I will see what can be done."

With that he rose and went to his own apartment and took out a little casket. Into the casket he put a fan, and shutting it up carefully, he brought it to the messenger and said, "Here is a casket. It has neither lock nor key and yet will open only to the touch of the person who needs its contents—and whoever opens it will obtain patience, but I cannot tell whether it will be the kind of patience that is wanted."

The servant bowed low and took the casket, but when he asked what was to be paid, the king would take nothing. So he went away and gave the casket and an account of his adventures to his master.

As soon as their father returned to his country, Kupti and Imani each received the presents he had brought for them. Imani was very surprised when the casket was brought to her by the hand of a messenger.

"But," she said, "what is this? I never asked for anything! Indeed I had no time, for the messenger ran away before I had unraveled my tangle."

But the servant declared the casket was for her, so she took it with some curiosity and brought it to the old beggar. The old man tried to open it, but in vain—so closely did the lid fit that it seemed to be quite immovable, and yet there was neither lock nor bolt nor spring, nor anything apparently by which the casket was kept shut. When he was tired of trying, he handed the casket to the princess, who hardly touched it before it opened quite easily, and there lay within a beautiful fan. With a cry of surprise and pleasure Imani took out the fan and began to fan herself.

Hardly had she finished three strokes of the fan before there suddenly appeared before her King Subbar Khan of Dûr! The princess gasped and rubbed her eyes, and the old beggar sat and gazed in such astonishment that for some minutes he could not speak.

At length he said, "Who may you be, fair sir, if you please?"

"My name," said the king, "is Subbar Khan of Dûr. This lady," bowing to the princess, "has summoned me, and here I am!"

"I?" stammered the princess. "I have summoned you? I never saw or heard of you in my life before, so how could that be?"

Then the king told them how he had heard of a man in his own city of Dûr trying to buy patience, and how he had given him the fan in the casket.

"Both are magical," he added. "When anyone uses the fan, in three strokes of it I am with her; if she folds it and taps it on the table, in three taps I am at home again. The casket will not open to all, but you see it was this fair lady who asked for patience, and as that is my name, here I am, very much at her service."

Now Princess Imani, being of a high spirit, was anxious to fold up the fan and give the three taps which would send the king home again. But the old man was very pleased with his guest, and so in one way and another they spent a pleasant evening together before Subbar Khan took his leave.

After that he was often summoned, and as both the beggar man and he were very fond of chess and were good players, they used to sit up half the night playing until at last a little room in the house began to be called the king's room. Whenever he stayed late he slept there and went home again in the morning.

By and by, it came to the ears of Princess Kupti that a rich and handsome young man was visiting at her sister's house, and she was very jealous. So she went one day to pay Imani a visit, pretending to be very affectionate and interested in the house, and in the way in which Imani and the old man lived, and of their mysterious and royal visitor.

As the sisters went from place to place, Kupti was shown Subbar Khan's room. Presently, making some excuse, she slipped in by herself and swiftly spread under the sheet, which lay upon the bed, a quantity of very finely powdered and splintered glass that was poisoned, and which she had brought with her concealed in her clothes. Shortly afterward she took leave of her sister, declaring she could never forgive herself for not having come near her all this time, and that she would now begin to make amends for her neglect.

That very evening Subbar Khan came and sat up late with the old man playing chess as usual. Very tired, he at length bade him and the princess good night, but as soon as he lay down on the bed, thou-

sands of tiny, tiny splinters of poisoned glass ran into him. He could not think what was the matter, and turned this way and that until he was pricked all over and felt as though he were burning from head to foot. But he said never a word, only sitting up all night in agony of body and in worse agony of mind to think that he should have been poisoned, as he guessed he was, in Imani's own house.

In the morning, although he was nearly fainting, he still said nothing, and by means of the magic fan was duly transported home again. Then he sent for all the physicians and doctors in his kingdom, but none could make out what his illness was. And so he lingered on for weeks and weeks, trying every remedy that anyone could devise, and passing sleepless nights and days of pain and fever and misery, until at last he was at the point of death.

Meanwhile Princess Imani and the old man were much troubled, because, although they waved the magic fan again and again, no Subbar Khan appeared. They feared that he had tired of them or that some evil fate had overtaken him. At last the princess was in such a miserable state of doubt and uncertainty that she determined to go herself to the kingdom of Dûr and see what was the matter. Disguising herself as a young beggar man, she set out upon her journey alone and on foot, as a beggar should travel.

One evening she found herself in a forest and lay down under a great tree to pass the night. But she could not sleep for thinking of Subbar Khan and wondering what had happened to him. Presently she heard two great monkeys talking to one another in the tree above her head.

"Good evening, brother," said one, "whence come you and what is the news?"

"I come from Dûr," said the other, "and the news is that the king is dying."

"Oh," said the first, "I'm sorry to hear that, for he is a master hand at slaying leopards and creatures that ought not to be allowed to live. What is the matter with him?"

"No man knows," replied the second monkey, "but the birds, who see all and carry all messages, say that he is dying of poisoned glass that Kupti, the king's daughter, spread upon his bed."

"Ah," said the first monkey, "that is sad news. But if they only knew it, the berries of the very tree we sit in, steeped in hot water, will cure such a disease as that in three days at most."

"True!" said the other. "It is a pity we cannot tell someone of a medicine so simple, and so save a good man's life. But people are so silly; they go and shut themselves up in stuffy houses in stuffy cities instead of living in nice airy trees, and so they miss knowing all the best things."

Now when Imani heard that Subbar Khan was dying, she began to weep silently. But as she listened, she dried her tears and sat up, and as soon as daylight dawned over the forest, she began to gather the berries from the tree until she had filled her cloth with a load of them. Then she walked on as fast as she could and in two days reached the city of Dûr.

The first thing she did was to pass through the market crying, "Medicine for sale! Are any ill that need my medicine?"

And presently one man said to his neighbor, "See, there is a young man with medicine for sale. Perhaps he could do something for the king."

"Pooh," replied the other, "where so many gray-beards have failed, how should a lad like that be of any use?"

"Still," said the first, "he might try." And he went up and spoke to Imani, and together they set out for the palace and announced that another doctor had come to try and cure the king.

 After some delay Imani was admitted to the sick room, and, while she was so well disguised that the king did not recognize her, he was so wasted by illness that she hardly knew him. But she began at once, full of hope, by asking for an apartment all to herself and a pot in which to boil water.

As soon as the water was heated she steeped some of her berries in it and, giving the mixture to the king's attendants, told them to wash his body with it. The first washing did so much good that the king slept quietly all the night. Again the second day she did the same, and this time the king declared he was hungry and called for food. After the third day he was quite well, only very weak from his long illness. On the fourth day he got up and sat upon his throne, and then sent messengers to fetch the physician who had cured him.

When Imani appeared, everyone marveled that so young a man should be so clever a doctor, and the king wanted to give him immense presents of money and of all kinds of precious things. At first Imani would take nothing, but at last she said that, if she must be rewarded, she would ask for the king's signet ring and his handkerchief. So, as she would take nothing more, the king gave her his signet ring and his handkerchief, and she departed and traveled back to her own country as fast as she could.

A little while after her return, when she had related to the old man all her adventures, they sent for Subbar Khan by means of the magic fan. When he appeared they asked him why he had stayed away for so long. Then he told them all about his illness and how he had been cured. When he had finished, the princess rose up and, opening a cabinet, brought out the ring and handkerchief and said, laughing, "Are these the rewards you gave to your doctor?"

At that the king recognized her and understood in a moment all that had happened, and he jumped up and put the magic fan in his pocket, declaring that no one should send him away to his own country anymore unless Imani would come with him and be his wife. And so it was settled, and the old beggar man and Imani went to the city of Dûr, where Imani was married to the king and lived happily ever after.

LEONORA BLANCHE ALLEYNE LANG *adapted this story from an old tale of the Punjabi area. It appeared in Andrew Lang's* Olive Fairy Book *(1907).*

The
LUTE
PLAYER

Once upon a time a king and a queen lived quite happily in their small kingdom. The king held tournaments and practiced mock battle with his knights, but after a time he grew bored and restless. He longed to go out into the world to try his skill in battle and to win fame and glory.

So he called his band of armed knights together and gave orders to start for a distant country where a cruel king who raided the countries all around him lived. The queen, who had always shared the duties of the kingdom, was now given full power to rule in his absence. He commanded his ministers to assist the queen in all things; then, taking tender leave of his wife, the king set out with his small force.

After a time the king reached the lands of the foreign ruler. He rode on until he came to a mountain pass where a large army lay in wait for him. His force was defeated; the king himself was taken prisoner.

He was carried off to the prison where the captives suffered badly. The prisoners were kept chained all night long, and in the morning they were yoked together like oxen to plow the land till it grew dark.

In the meantime the queen governed the land wisely and well. The country remained at peace with its neighbors and her subjects prospered. But when one year became two, and then three, the queen grieved at her husband's long absence. Since no word was received from him, she feared he had been killed.

When at last the poor king was able to send her a message, her grief turned to joy. The letter told of his capture and gave instructions for his rescue:

". . . Sell our castles and estates and borrow money to raise as large a fortune as you can. Either bring or send the gold to ransom me—for that is the only hope of deliverance from this terrible prison . . ."

The queen pondered the message. She was resolved to obtain his release as quickly as possible, but to raise so large a sum would take many months.

"Then if I bring the ransom gold myself," she thought, "this foreign king might seize the gold and imprison me, too. If I send messengers with the ransom, whom shall I trust? It is a long distance to travel with a cart full of gold! And what then if the ransom offer is refused or seized? This ruthless king may not want to ransom a prisoner—or he may be so wealthy he will laugh at our gold!"

The queen paced her chamber in despair. "If I do as the king requests, he would return home beggared and in debt, the country impoverished." These thoughts filled her mind until she was nearly distracted.

At last an idea came to her. She would journey to the distant land as a vagabond minstrel, a lute player, and she would rescue the king herself. She cut her long brown hair and dressed herself as a minstrel boy. Then she took her lute, and leaving word that she was going on a journey, she left the castle at night. She did not know if her bold plan would succeed, but she knew the ministers would be horrified and detain her if they could.

At first the queen rode alone, but soon she joined a party of pilgrims journeying her way. Later she joined a group of merchants and peddlers. The young minstrel who played the lute so well and sang so gaily was welcome company to the travelers.

In this way she neared her destination in little more than a month. Leaving the party of merchants, she headed for the steep mountain pass and the country where her husband was imprisoned. She had become thin and browned by the sun, and the bright colors of her minstrel cloak were dusty and worn.

When at last she arrived at the palace of the foreign king, she walked all around it and at the back she saw the prison. Then she went into the great court in front of the palace. Taking her lute in her hands, she began to play so artfully that all who heard her felt as though they could never hear enough.

After she had played for some time she began to sing, and her voice was sweeter than the nightingale's:

> *I come from my own country far*
> *Into this foreign land;*
> *Of all I own, I take alone*
> *My sweet lute in my hand.*
>
> *Oh, who will thank me for my song*
> *Reward my simple lay?* *
> *Like lovers' sighs it still shall rise*
> *To greet thee day by day.*

*A lay is a ballad or song.

My song begs for your pity
And gifts from out your store;
And as I play my gentle lay
I linger near your door.

And if you hear my singing
Within your palace, sire,
Oh, give I pray, this happy day,
To me my heart's desire.

No sooner had the king heard this touching song, sung by such a lovely voice, than he had the singer brought before him.

"Welcome, lute player," said he. "Where do you come from?"

"My country, sire, is far away across many lands. I wander from country to country, and I earn my living with my music."

"Stay here then a few days, and when you wish to leave, I will give you as reward what you ask for in your song—your heart's desire."

So the lute player stayed on in the palace and played and sang songs both merry and sad. The king, who was charmed and beguiled by the songs and the music, never tired of listening and almost forgot to eat or drink.

After three days the lute player came to take leave of the king.

"Well," said the king, "what do you desire as your reward?"

"Sire, give me one of your prisoners. You have so many in your prison, and I should be glad of a companion on my journeys. When I hear his happy voice as I travel along, I shall think of you and thank you."

"Come along then," said the king, "choose whomever you wish." And he took the lute player through the prison himself.

The queen walked about among the prisoners, and at length she picked out her husband and took him with her on her journey home. Again they traveled the roads with parties of pilgrims and traders, and the king never suspected that the thin, sun-browned minstrel who entertained the travelers could be his queen.

At last they reached the border of their own country. "Let me go now, kind lad," said her companion. "I am no common prisoner but the king of this country. Let me go free and ask what you will as your reward."

"Do not speak of reward," answered the lute player. "Go in peace."

"Then come with me, friend, and be my guest."

"When the proper time comes I shall be at your palace," said the minstrel, and so they parted.

The queen took a shorter way home, arriving at the castle before the king. She changed her clothes, putting on her most splendid gown and a high silk headdress.

An hour later, all the people in the castle were running to the courtyard crying, "Our king has come back! After three long years, our king has returned!"

The king greeted everyone kindly, but to his queen he said reproachfully, "Did you not receive my message? I lay a long time in prison waiting to be ransomed! Now you greet me lovingly, but it was a young lute player who rescued me and brought me home!"

The queen had expected to tell the king in the privacy of their chamber the reasons for her disguise and perilous journey, for she feared he would be angry that she had not sent the ransom money. But before she could make a suitable reply, a spiteful minister standing nearby said, "Sire, when news of your imprisonment arrived, the queen left the castle and only returned today."

At this the king looked stricken and sorrowful. He turned away to confer with his ministers, for he thought the queen had deserted him in his time of need. The queen returned to her chamber and put on again her travel-stained minstrel cloak and hood. Taking her lute, she slipped down to the castle courtyard where she sang, in a sweet clear voice, the verses she had sung in the far-off land:

> *I sing the captive's longing*
> *Within his prison wall,*
> *Of hearts that sigh when none are nigh*
> *To answer to their call.*

> *And if you hear my singing*
> *Within your palace, sire,*
> *Oh give, I pray, this happy day,*
> *To me my heart's desire.*

As soon as the king heard this song he ran out to meet the lute player, took him by the hand, and led him into the castle.

"Here," he cried, "is the boy who released me from my prison. And now, my true friend, I will indeed give you your heart's desire."

"I ask only your trust and love," said she, throwing off the hooded cloak and revealing herself as the queen. "And I beg that you listen to my story."

A cry of astonishment rang through the hall. The king stood amazed, then rushed to embrace her.

"My dear husband," said the queen as she led him to one side, "I did receive your message, but

I chose to follow another plan." Then the queen told him all that had troubled her about the ransom plan, and why she thought it the wiser course to rescue the king, instead, through her skill as a lute player.

"Thus," she ended, "you return not to a sorry kingdom of debts and people overburdened with taxes, but to a prosperous land and contented subjects."

Then the king rejoiced in the wisdom and courage of the queen and, in gratitude, proclaimed a seven-day feast of celebration throughout the land.

DOROTHY BLACKLEY *contributed this story to Andrew Lang's* The Violet Fairy Book *(1901) with a note that it had a Russian source. However, the story seems to have a general European locale. The idea of using a minstrel disguise for gaining safe access to a palace or king was used in tales of the thirteenth century. This retelling by the editor somewhat expands Blackley's nineteenth-century story.*

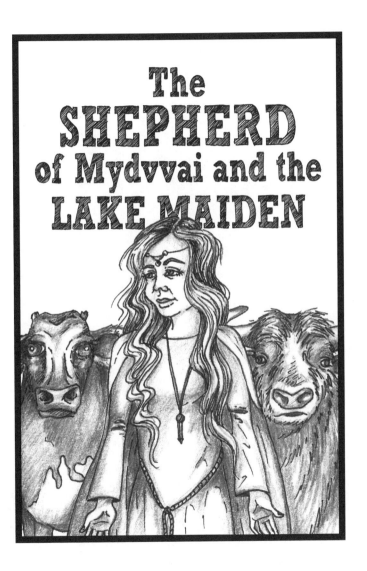

The
SHEPHERD
of Mydvvai and the
LAKE MAIDEN

Long, long ago in the mountains of Wales, there lived a young shepherd lad with his mother. They lived in the wide sloping valley, and every day the lad drove his flock up through the rocky pass to the fine pasture land surrounding a clear blue lake.

He was a quiet lad given to dreaming as the flocks grazed and fashioning light airy tunes on the reed pipes he carried. It was a simple life, and although his mother sometimes sighed and wished the lad were more ambitious, still they did have a snug cottage and healthy livestock.

One day, at midsummer, the shepherd was resting in the shade and unwrapping the round, hard-baked barley loaf his mother had packed for him. Suddenly three maidens rose up from the waters of the lake, glided to shore, and wandered among the wild flowers. Each had long golden hair and moved with an airy grace that was a joy to behold. One of the maidens came close to where the shepherd lay quite still with wonder. Her face, indeed her whole being, shone with a radiance that was scarcely human.

The lad spoke to her and shyly offered her his bread. The maiden took the loaf and tried it. Then she gave it back and sang,

> *Hard, too hard is thy bread;*
> *That will never feed me.*

And she ran off laughing into the waters of the lake.

That evening the lad returned home with his flock and hurried in to tell his mother about the strange and wonderful happening.

"She was that radiant and merry," said the lad at the end, "I fell in love with her. I'll have no other for my wife!"

"'Tis bewitched you are!" said his mother, shaking her head. Then she added briskly, "Your bread was too hard for her, was it? I'll mix up more dough and bake it soft, but I doubt you'll see her again."

Nonetheless the shepherd lad did see her again the very next day. This time the Lake Maiden came forth alone, and in the lad's eyes she shone as radiantly as dew in the morning sun. They walked together by the shore of the lake, and the shepherd told her he loved her. He said he would marry no one but her.

But when he offered her the soft bread, she tried it, then sang,

> *Unbaked is thy bread,*
> *I will not have thee.*

With a mocking laugh the maiden ran lightly back to the waters of the lake and disappeared.

When he returned home with his flock that evening, the lad told his mother the bread was too soft. "Unbaked, she called it," he said in despair.

"We'll try again," said his mother getting out her finest ground flour. And this time she baked a perfect loaf for her son to take with him. It was crisp on the outside, light and well-baked within.

 Long and anxiously he waited the next day until he feared she would not come at all. On his reed pipes he played the airy tunes she liked and then a plaintive melody to tell his heart's longing. Toward evening the maiden rose from the lake and came toward him.

The shepherd hastened to meet her. Humbly he offered the round baked loaf. On an impulse he sprinkled the offering with a few drops of lake water.

The Lake Maiden tasted the bread. Smiling, she said she would leave the lake and dwell with him. Then she raised her arm toward the lake and beckoned. Up from the water rose several sleek cows, a bull, and two oxen. They splashed ashore and stood behind her.

"There is one condition," said she. "You must never touch me with anything made of iron. For if you do, I cannot stay with you no matter how much I may want to. I must return to the lake with my cattle, and you will never see me again."

Joyfully the shepherd agreed. "That will be an easy condition to remember," he answered. "I will never let anything made of iron touch you." Proudly he led home his bride and the herd of fairy cattle.

They lived happily together for many years. Two sons and a daughter were born to them and grew up to be strong, healthy, and wise. In that part of Wales, no one had ever seen so much milk, or tasted such fine butter and cheese as came from the fairy cows. The family had good fortune with all their livestock and became prosperous.

Now as the years passed, the shepherd grew old

and gray—but the Lake Maiden never seemed to change. She still had the same radiant appearance as the first day she rose from the waters of the lake.

One day the husband and wife went out to the hillside to catch some ponies, for they planned to ride into market. The wife was still as fleet as a girl, and in a few minutes she had caught a pony by the mane.

"Throw me the halter," she called.

But the husband, without thinking, threw the bridle, and the iron bit struck his wife's hand.

The Lake Maiden let go the pony and stood for a moment looking at him sadly. Then she sang,

Brindle cow, white speckled,
Spotted cow, bold freckled;
Old Whiteface, and gray Berenger,
The white bull, the gray ox,
And the black calf, come!
All come and follow me home.

The sky grew dark, the wind lashed the trees. The Lake Maiden walked back up the mountain. All the fairy cattle and their offspring followed her—

the cows from the byre, the bulls from the pasture, the oxen with the plows still dragging behind them. The Lake Maiden entered the lake, her fairy cattle behind her.

The old shepherd went back to the house and wept. He called in his family and told them all that had happened, for they had never heard the story of their mother before.

The brothers and sister believed their mother might be seen again. Every evening they climbed up the rocky track to watch patiently by the shore of the lake. But the lake was still and calm, week after week, with only a breeze faintly stirring the surface.

At last one evening when the sun was lying low in the west, and all three were watching quietly, the Lake Maiden rose out of the water and came to them.

"I will always love you, and I will always watch over you," she said. "I will watch over your children's children, and those who come after them. This one last time I have come back to teach you all the healing charms."

Then she walked with them through the meadows, showing them where all the healing plants grew: one for eye infections, one for fever, another for healing all wounds. She taught them when and how to gather the plants, how to boil and prepare them.

So much of the art of healing did she teach them before she returned to the lake, that these three became the wisest and the most skilled physicians in Wales. They taught all these things to their daughters and to their sons. In this way the knowledge and the art of healing was passed to their children's children, and to each new generation long into time.

Their extraordinary powers of healing brought fame and renown to the family, and for hundreds of years people came to the village of Myddvai from all over Wales to be healed. For this was the legacy given to her family and their descendants by the Lake Maiden.

In Wales, the Lake Maiden was once a local goddess, and the physicians of Myddvai came from an actual family renowned for their medical skill for the six centuries before the family died out in 1743. There are different versions of this tale, but all have basically the same plot. This retelling by the editor is from a story in **JOSEPH JACOBS**'s Celtic Fairy Tales *(1892).*

The Search
for the
MAGIC
LAKE

Long ago there was a ruler of the vast Inca Empire who had an only son. This youth brought great joy to his father's heart but also a sadness, for the prince had been born in ill health.

As the years passed the prince's health did not improve, and none of the court doctors could find a cure for his illness.

One night the aged emperor went down on his knees and prayed at the altar.

"Oh Great Ones," he said, "I am getting older and will soon leave my people and join you in the heavens. There is no one to look after them but my son, the prince. I pray you make him well and strong so he can be a fit ruler for my people. Tell me how his malady can be cured."

The emperor put his head in his hands and waited for an answer. Soon he heard a voice coming from the fire that burned constantly in front of the altar.

"Let the prince drink water from the magic lake at the end of the world," the voice said, "and he will be well."

At that moment the fire sputtered and died. Among the cold ashes lay a golden flask.

But the emperor was much too old to make the long journey to the end of the world, and the young prince was too ill to travel. So the emperor proclaimed that whoever should fill the golden flask with the magic water would be greatly rewarded.

Many brave men set out to search for the magic lake, but none could find it. Days and weeks passed and still the flask remained empty.

In a valley, some distance from the emperor's palace, lived a poor farmer who had a wife, two grown sons, and a young daughter.

One day the older son said to his father, "Let my brother and me join in the search for the magic lake. Before the moon is new again, we shall return and help you harvest the corn and potatoes."

The father remained silent. He was not thinking of the harvest, but feared for his sons' safety.

When the father did not answer, the second son added, "Think of the rich reward, Father!"

"It is their duty to go," said his wife, "for we must all try to help our emperor and the young prince."

After his wife had spoken, the father yielded.

"Go, if you must, but beware of the wild beasts and evil spirits," he cautioned.

With their parents' blessing, and an affectionate farewell from their young sister, the sons set out on their journey.

They found many lakes, but none where the sky touched the water.

Finally the younger brother said, "Before another day has passed we must return to help father with the harvest."

"Yes," agreed the other, "but I have thought of a plan. Let us each carry a jar of water from any lake along the way. We can say it will cure the prince. Even if it doesn't, surely the emperor will give us a small reward for our trouble."

"Agreed," said the younger brother.

On arriving at the palace, the youths told the emperor and his court that they brought water from the magic lake. At once the prince was given a sip from each of the brothers' jars, but of course he remained as ill as before.

"Perhaps the water must be sipped from the golden flask," one of the high priests said.

But the golden flask would not hold the water. In

some mysterious way, the water from the jars disappeared as soon as it was poured into the flask.

In despair the emperor called for his magician and said to him, "Can you break the spell of the flask so the water will remain for my son to drink?"

"I cannot do that, your majesty," replied the magician. "But I believe," he added wisely, "that the flask is telling us that we have been deceived by the two brothers. The flask can be filled only with water from the magic lake."

When the brothers heard this, they trembled with fright, for they knew their falsehood was discovered.

So angry was the emperor that he ordered the brothers thrown into chains. Each day they were forced to drink water from their jars as a reminder of their false deed. News of their disgrace spread far and wide.

Again the emperor sent messengers throughout the land pleading for someone to bring the magic water before death claimed him and the young prince.

Súmac, the little sister of the youths, was tending her flock of llamas when she heard the sound of the royal trumpet. Then came the voice of the emperor's servant with his urgent message from the court.

Quickly the child led her llamas home and begged her parents to let her go in search of the magic water.

"You are too young," her father said. "Besides, look at what has already befallen your brothers. Some evil spirit must have taken hold of them to make them tell such a lie."

And her mother said, "We could not bear to be without our precious Súmac!"

"But think how sad our emperor will be if the young prince dies," replied Súmac. "And if I can find the magic lake, perhaps the emperor will forgive my brothers and send them home."

"Dear husband," said Súmac's mother, "maybe it is the will of the gods that we let her go."

Once again the father gave his permission.

Súmac was overjoyed and went skipping out to the corral to harness one of her pet llamas. It would carry her provisions and keep her company.

Meanwhile her mother filled a little woven bag with food and drink for Súmac—toasted golden kernels of corn and a little earthen jar of *chicha*, a beverage made from crushed corn.

The three embraced each other tearfully before Súmac set out bravely on her mission, leading her pet llama along the trail.

The first night she slept, snug and warm against her llama, in the shelter of a few rocks. But when she heard the hungry cry of the puma, she feared for her pet animal and bade it return safely home.

The next night she spent in the top branches of a tall tree, far out of reach of the dreadful puma. She hid her provisions in a hole in the tree trunk.

At sunrise she was aroused by the voices of gentle sparrows resting on a nearby limb.

"Poor child," said the oldest sparrow, "she can never find her way to the lake."

"Let us help her," chorused the others.

"Oh please do!" implored the child, "and forgive me for intruding in your tree."

"We welcome you," chirped another sparrow, "for you are the same little girl who yesterday shared your golden corn with us."

 "We shall help you," continued the first sparrow, who was the leader, "for you are a good child. Each of us will give you a wing feather, and you must hold them all together in one hand as a fan. The feathers have magic powers that will carry you wherever you wish to go. They will also protect you from harm."

Each sparrow then lifted a wing, sought out a special feather hidden underneath, and gave it to Súmac. She fashioned them into the shape of a little fan, taking the ribbon from her hair to bind the feathers together so that none would be lost.

"I must warn you," said the oldest sparrow, "that the lake is guarded by three terrible creatures. But have no fear. Hold the magic fan up to your face and you will be unharmed."

Súmac thanked the birds over and over again. Then, holding up the fan in her hands she said politely, "Please magic fan, take me to the lake at the end of the world."

A soft breeze swept her out of the top branches of the tree and through the valley. Then up she was carried, higher and higher into the sky, until she could look down and see the great mountain peaks covered with snow.

At last the wind put her down on the shore of a beautiful lake. It was, indeed, the lake at the end of the world, for, on the opposite side from where she stood, the sky came down so low it touched the water.

Súmac tucked the magic fan into her waistband and ran to the edge of the water. Suddenly her face fell. She had left everything back in the forest. What could she use for carrying the precious water back to the prince?

"Oh, I do wish I had remembered the jar!" she said.

Suddenly she heard a soft thud in the sand at her

feet. She looked down and discovered a beautiful golden flask—the same one the emperor had found in the ashes.

Súmac took the flask and kneeled at the water's edge. Just then a hissing voice behind her said, "Get away from my lake or I shall wrap my long, hairy legs around your neck."

Súmac turned around. There stood a giant crab as large as a pig and as black as night.

With trembling hands the child took the magic fan from her waistband and spread it open in front of her face. As soon as the crab looked at it, he closed his eyes and fell down on the sand in a deep sleep.

Once more Súmac started to fill the flask. This time she was startled by a fierce voice bubbling up from the water.

"Get away from my lake or I shall eat you," gurgled a giant green alligator. His long tail beat the water angrily.

Súmac waited until the creature swam closer. Then she held up the fan. The alligator blinked. He drew back. Slowly, quietly, he sank to the bottom of the lake in a sound sleep.

Before Súmac could recover from her fright, she heard a shrill whistle in the air. She looked up and saw a flying serpent. His skin was red as blood. Sparks flew from his eyes.

"Get away from my lake or I shall bite you," hissed the serpent as it batted its wings around her head.

Again Súmac's fan saved her from harm. The serpent closed his eyes and drifted to the ground. He folded his wings and coiled up on the sand. Then he began to snore.

Súmac sat for a moment to quiet herself. Then, realizing that the danger was past, she sighed with great relief.

"Now I can fill the golden flask and be on my way," she said to herself.

When this was done, she held the flask tightly in one hand and clutched the fan in the other.

"Please take me to the palace," she said.

Hardly were the words spoken, when she found herself safely in front of the palace gates. She looked at the tall guard.

"I wish to see the emperor," Súmac uttered in trembling tones.

"Why, little girl?" the guard asked kindly.

"I bring water from the magic lake to cure the prince."

The guard looked down at her in astonishment.

"Come!" he commanded in a voice loud and deep as thunder.

In just a few moments Súmac was led into a room full of sadness. The emperor was pacing up and down in despair. The prince lay motionless on a huge bed. His eyes were closed and his face was without color. Beside him knelt his mother, weeping.

Without wasting words, Súmac went to the prince and gave him a few drops of magic water. Soon he opened his eyes. His cheeks became flushed. It was not long before he sat up in bed. He drank some more.

"How strong I feel!" the prince cried joyfully.

The emperor and his wife embraced Súmac.

Then Súmac told them of her adventurous trip to the lake. They praised her courage. They marveled at the reappearance of the golden flask and at the powers of the magic fan.

"Dear child," said the emperor, "all the riches of my empire are not enough to repay you for saving my son's life. Ask what you will and it shall be yours."

"Oh, generous emperor," said Súmac timidly, "I have but three wishes."

"Name them and they shall be yours," urged the emperor.

"First, I wish my brothers to be free to return to my parents. They have learned their lesson and will never be false again. I know they were only thinking of a reward for my parents. Please forgive them."

"Guards, free them at once!" ordered the emperor.

"Secondly, I wish the magic fan returned to the forest so the sparrows may have their feathers again."

This time the emperor had no time to speak. Before anyone in the room could utter a sound, the magic fan lifted itself up, spread itself wide open, and floated out the window toward the woods. Everyone watched in amazement. When the fan was out of sight, they applauded.

"What is your last wish, dear Súmac?" asked the queen mother.

"I wish that my parents be given a large farm and great flocks of llamas, vicuñas, and alpacas, so they will not be poor any longer."

"It will be so," said the emperor, "but I am sure your parents never considered themselves poor with so wonderful a daughter."

"Won't you stay with us in the palace?" ventured the prince.

"Yes, stay with us!" urged his father and mother. "We will do everything to make you happy."

"Oh thank you," said Súmac happily, "but I must return to my parents and my brothers. I miss them as I know they have missed me. They do not even know I am safe, for I came directly to your palace."

The royal family did not try to detain Súmac any longer.

"My own guard will see that you get home safely," said the emperor.

When she reached home, she found that all she had wished for had come to pass: her brothers were waiting for her with their parents; a beautiful house and huge barn were being constructed; and her father had received a deed granting him many acres of new, rich farmland.

Súmac ran into the arms of her happy family.

This tale is reprinted from **GENEVIEVE BARLOW**'s Latin American Tales *(1966) and was told to the author by Incas living in Ecuador. The Inca Empire, which originated in Peru, extended over Ecuador and other parts of South America during the fifteenth and sixteenth centuries.*

The
Squire's
BRIDE

There was once a very rich squire who owned a large farm and had plenty of silver in his money chest and gold in the bank, but there was something he had not, and that was a wife.

One day a neighbor's daughter was working for the squire in the hayfield. He liked her very much, and as she was a poor farmer's daughter, the squire thought that if he only mentioned marriage she would be more than glad to accept at once.

So he said to her, "I've been thinking I want to marry."

"Well, one may think of many things," said the lassie as she stood there. She really thought the old fellow ought to be thinking of something that suited him better than getting married to a young lass at his time of life.

"I was thinking that you should be my wife!" said he.

"No, thank you," said she, "and much obliged for the honor."

The squire was not used to being refused, and the more she refused him, the more he wanted her. But the lassie would not listen to him at all. So the old squire sent for her father. He told the farmer to talk to his daughter and arrange the marriage. Then the squire would forgive the farmer the money he had lent him and would give him the piece of land that lay close to his meadow in the bargain.

"Yes, yes, be sure I'll bring the lass to her senses," said the father. "She is young and does not know what is best for her."

But all his coaxing, all his threats, and all his talking went for naught. She said she would not have the old miser, if he sat buried in gold up to his ears.

The squire waited and waited, but at last he got angry. The next day he visited the poor farmer and told him that he had to settle the matter at once if he expected the squire to stand by his bargain. For now he would wait no longer to be married.

The farmer knew no other way out but to agree to let the squire get everything ready for the wedding. Then, when the parson and the wedding guests had arrived, the squire would send for the lassie as if she were wanted for some work.

When she reached him, the squire thought, she would be so awed by the fine bridal clothes and the wedding guests that she would agree to be married, for he could not believe a farm girl would really refuse a rich husband.

When the guests had arrived, the squire called one of his farm lads and told him to run down to his neighbor to ask him to send up immediately what he had promised.

"But if you are not back with her in a twinkling," he said, shaking his fist at him, "I'll . . ."

He did not finish, for the lad ran off as if he had been shot at from behind.

"My master has sent me to ask for that which you promised him," said the lad, when he got to the neighbor. "But pray, lose no time, for master is terribly busy today."

"Yes, yes, run down in the meadow and take her with you," answered the girl's father.

The lad ran off and when he came to the meadow, he found the daughter raking hay.

"I am to fetch what your father has promised my master," said the lad.

"Aha!" thought she. "Is that what they are up to?" And with a twinkle in her eye she said, "Oh yes, it's that little bay mare of ours, I suppose. You had better go and take her. She stands grazing on the other side of the pea field."

The boy jumped on the back of the horse and rode her home at a full gallop.

"Have you got her with you?" asked the squire.

"She is down at the door," said the lad.

"Take her up to the room my mother had," said the squire.

"But master, how can I?" said the lad.

"Do as I tell you!" roared the old squire. "And if you can't persuade her, get someone to help you!"

When the lad saw his master's face, he knew it would be no use to argue. So he went and got all the farm hands together to help him. Some pulled at the head of the mare, and others pushed from behind, and at last they got her upstairs and into the room where they tied the reins to a bedpost. The wedding finery, with the crown and flowered wreath, was spread out on the bed all ready for the bride.

"Well, that's done, master," said the lad when he returned. He mopped his brow. "That was the hardest job I've ever had here on the farm."

"Never mind, never mind, you shall not have done it for nothing," said the master. He pulled a silver coin out of his pocket and gave it to the lad. "Now send the women up to dress her."

"But, I say, master. How can they?"

"None of your talk," cried the squire. "Tell them to dress her in the wedding clothes, and mind not to forget either wreath or crown!"

The lad ran into the kitchen. "Listen here, lasses," he called out. "The master's gone daft! You are to go upstairs and dress up the bay mare as a bride. I suppose he wants to play a joke on his guests!"

The women laughed and laughed, but ran upstairs and dressed the horse in all the finery that was there. And then the lad went and told his master that now all was ready, complete with wreath and crown.

"Very well, bring her down. I will meet her at the door myself," said the squire.

There was a loud clatter and thumping on the stairs as the mare was led down. Then the door was thrown open to the large room where the squire waited with the wedding guests.

In walked the bay mare dressed as a bride, with a wreath of flowers falling over one eye. The parson gaped in astonishment. The guests broke into loud laughter, and as for the squire—they say he never went courting again.

Norwegian folktales often have an earthy humor. **GUDRUN THORNE-THOMSEN**'s *translation (1912) is the source for this retelling by the editor.*

There once was a girl who wanted to touch the stars in the sky.

On clear nights, when she looked through her bedroom window, the stars twinkled and glittered in the velvet blackness of the sky above. Sometimes the stars seemed like diamonds, sometimes like tears, and sometimes like merry eyes.

One summer evening the lass set off to seek the stars. She walked and walked until she came to the dark, satiny surface of a millpond.

"Good evening," said she. "I'm seeking the stars in the sky. Can you help me?"

"They're right here," murmured the pond. "They shine so brightly on my face that I can't sleep nights. Jump in, lass. See if you can catch one."

The lass jumped into the pond and swam all around it. But never a star did she find.

She walked on across the fields until she came to a chattering brook.

"Good evening," said she. "I'm off to find the stars in the sky. Do you know how to reach them?"

"Yes, yes. They're always dancing about on the stones and water here," chattered the brook. "Come in and catch one if you can."

The lass waded in, but not a star could she find in the brook.

"I don't think the stars come down here at all!" she cried.

"Well, they *look* as if they're here," said the brook pertly. "And isn't that the same thing?"

"Not the same thing at all," said the girl.

She walked on until she met a host of Little Folk dancing on the grass. No taller than herself, they seemed very elegant in their clothes of green and gold.

"Good evening to you, Little Folk of the Hill," she called, taking care to be polite. "I'm seeking the stars in the sky."

High, silvery voices rang out. "They shine on the grass here at night. Come dance with us if you want to find one."

The lass joined the round ring dance of the Little Folk and danced and danced. But although the grass twinkled and gleamed beneath their feet, not a star did she find.

She left the dancers and sat down beyond the ring. "I've searched and searched, but there are no stars down here," she cried. "Can't you tell me how to reach the stars?"

The dancers simply laughed. Then one of the company came over to her and said, "Since you're so set on it, I'll give you this advice. If you won't go back, go forward. Keep  going forward, and mind you take the right road. Ask Four-Feet to carry you to No-Feet-At-All. Then tell No-Feet-At-All to carry you to the Stairs without Steps. If you can climb them—"

"If I can, will I be up among the stars in the sky at last?" she asked.

"If you're not there, you'll be somewhere else," said the Little Man, and he ran back to join the dancers.

With a light heart, the lass stood up and went forward. Just as she was beginning to doubt that she was on the right road, she came to a silver-gray horse beneath a rowan tree.

"Good evening," said the lass. "I'm seeking the stars in the sky and my feet are weary. Will you carry me along the way?"

"I know nothing about stars in the sky," said the horse. "I am here to do the bidding of the Little Folk only."

"I've just been dancing with them, and I was told to ask Four-Feet to carry me to No-Feet-At-All."

"In that case, climb on my back," said the horse. "I am Four-Feet, and I will take you there."

They rode on and on until they left the woods behind and came to the edge of the land. Before them on the water, a wide, gleaming path of silver ran straight out to sea. And in the distance, a wonderful arch of brilliant colors rose from the water and went right up into the sky.

"I've brought you to the end of land," said the horse. "That's as much as Four-Feet can do for you. Climb down now; I must be off."

The lass slid from the horse and stood on the

shore, looking about her. A large fish swam in from the sea.

"Good evening, fish," she called. "I'm looking for the stars in the sky. Can you show me the way?"

"Not unless you bring the word of the Little Folk," said the fish.

"I can indeed," she answered. "Four-Feet brought me here, and I was told No-Feet-At-All would carry me to the Stairs without Steps."

"In that case," said the fish, "I will take you. Sit on my back and hold tight."

Off he swam with the girl on his back, straight along the silver path toward the bright arch of many colors. As they came to the foot of it, she saw the broad stairs of color rising steeply into the sky. At the far end of it were the merry, glittering stars.

"Here you are," said the fish. "These are the Stairs without Steps. They're not easy to climb. Climb if you can, but mind you hold fast and don't fall!"

So she started off. It was not easy at all to climb the bright-colored light. She climbed on and on, and it seemed she moved very slowly. Although she was high above the sea, the stars were still far away.

She was very weary but she thought, "I've come this far. I won't give up now."

On and on she went. The air grew colder, the

light more brilliant, until at last she reached the top of the arch. All about her the stars darted, raced, and spun in dazzling flashes of light. Below her, stretching down into darkness, were the brilliant colors of the Stairs without Steps.

She had reached the stars in the sky at last, and she stood transfixed with joy at the sheer wonder of it all.

After a time she became aware that the air was icy cold, and the hard, brilliant light of the spinning stars made her dizzy. Shading her eyes with her hand, she tried to see the earth below, but all was in darkness. No warm flicker of hearth or candlelight could be seen.

Then, in one last yearning effort, she stretched out her hand to touch a flashing star. She reached farther, farther—until suddenly she lost her balance. With a sigh—half of regret, half of contentment—she slid down, down, faster and faster into the darkness below, and all sense left her.

When she opened her eyes, it was morning. The sun shone warm and golden on her bed.

"I *did* reach the stars!" she thought with joy. But in the safe stillness of her room, she wondered, "Or did I dream it?"

Then she opened her tightly curled right hand, and on her palm lay a brilliant speck of stardust.

This tale was first collected by **JOSEPH JACOBS** *in* More English Fairy Tales, *published in 1894.*

BUCCA DHU and BUCCA GWIDDEN

You must know that there are two buccas.* Bucca Dhu is the bad goblin, and Bucca Gwidden is the good one. But Bucca Dhu is much bigger and stronger and fiercer than Bucca Gwidden, who is but a little meek thing, after all.

Now once upon a time there was a gay old woman who lived on a farm with her son and her daughter-in-law. The old woman was very fond of playing cards, and even of dancing and singing, though the son and the daughter-in-law thought she ought to know better at her time of life. Wherever people were gathered together to enjoy themselves, there the old woman would be: if it was card

---

* Buccas are mischievous spirits found in the folklore of Cornwall. They are similar to the pookas of Ireland and to the pixies and hobgoblins found in other parts of England.

playing, she would fling down her pennies and play with the rest; if it was dancing, she would tuck up her petticoats and foot it right merrily; and if it was singing, she would bawl away in her cracked voice, till she had everyone laughing.

When these parties were over and she set out to walk back to the farm, she would call at the inn on her way and take a glass or two of hot toddy to keep out the cold, and that made her sing all the louder. And so she would wander home, through dark night or clear night, or wet night or fine night, with her bonnet over one eye and her shawl trailing, and as merry as a cricket in the hedge.

The son didn't like it, nor yet did the daughter-in-law, for they were very proper sort of people.

"She puts us to shame," they said.

So they decided to give her such a fright that she would never venture out at night again.

One dark night, the daughter-in-law fetched a big sheet and put it over the son's head, and tied it round his neck and wrists. He couldn't see very well inside the sheet, so she took him by the hand and led him to a stile that the old woman had to pass over.

"Stay here by the brush," said the daughter-in-law, "and when your mother clambers up onto the top of the stile, jump out and wave your arms and groan. *That'll* scare her! She won't want to go over that stile at night again in a hurry!"

And she went back to the farm, and left him standing under the bush.

He waited a long time. It was a windy night, and the bush creaked and rustled and waved its branches about. The man soon began to wish himself safe home again. It seemed to him that there was something alive behind him in the bush, and he kept turning round, but he couldn't see with the sheet over his head. The more the bush creaked and rustled, the more certain he became that there was something lurking there. He began to think of all the tales he had heard about the bad Bucca Dhu, with his long claws to scratch with, and his great teeth to bite with, for it was just the kind of night when goblins are abroad.

Every minute that passed, the man was getting more and more fearful, and still there was no sign of the old woman. But at last he heard her coming along the path beyond the stile, hopping from one foot to the other, and singing,

> *On this black night there's nought to see*
> *But Bucca Dhu and me, and me!*

"Now keep thy distance, Bucca Dhu," she called over her shoulder. "I aren't afraid of 'ee!"

And so she scrambled up on the top of the stile.

When her son heard her speaking to Bucca Dhu, his teeth began to chatter, but he leaped out from the bush, and waved his arms inside the sheet, and groaned, just as the daughter-in-law had told him to do.

The old woman sat down on the stile and laughed.

"Well now," says she, "if it ain't good little Bucca Gwidden! But thou'st best run along home, my dear, for that old Bucca Dhu is a-following of me close, and if he catches thee, he'll tear thy eyes out! . . . Here he is, here he is!" she cried, turning to looking back over the stile. "He's getting bigger every minute, and he's in some rage! Run, Bucca Gwidden, run, run for thy life!"

Her son didn't wait to be told twice. He gathered up the sheet about his knees as well as he could, and he ran. And since he couldn't see where he was going, he bumped into trees, and stumbled over stones, and fell down, and scrambled up again, and stumbled again.

The old woman sat on the top of the stile and kicked with her heels and clapped with her hands.

"Run, Bucca Gwidden, run, run, run!" she

screamed. "After him, Bucca Dhu, catch him, boy, catch him! Well run, Bucca Gwidden, well run Bucca Dhu! Tear him, Bucca Dhu! Run, Bucca Gwidden!"

When the briars caught the sheet, the son thought it was Bucca Dhu's claws that were in him, and when he ran against the branches of a tree, he thought it was Bucca Dhu's arms that were round him; and all the while he ran, the old woman sat on the top of the stile and screamed for joy. He got home at last, more dead than alive, and the daughter-in-law had just taken the sheet off him, and sat him down before the fire to catch his breath, when the old woman walked in.

"Oh my, oh my, oh my!" says she. "*Such* goings on! I met with Bucca Dhu along the way, and we hadn't gone far together when out from a bush leaps Bucca Gwidden! And that great big bucca he set on the little bucca and chased him for his life! One ran, and t'other ran, and 'twas the merriest chase that ever I did see!"

"I can't tell 'ee if Bucca Dhu catched Bucca Gwidden—maybe he did, and maybe he didn't. Nor I can't exactly tell 'ee what Bucca Dhu was dressed in. But sure as I'm alive, Bucca Gwidden was wearing one of our sheets, and believe it or not, son, he had boots on just like thine!"

The son smirked, and the daughter-in-law looked foolish. They saw that the old woman was too clever for them, and they never tried to interfere with her again. So she lived merrily all her days.

The original source for this tale is **W. BOTTRELL**'s *nineteenth-century collection of Cornish folktales. The version used here is from* Peter and the Piskies *(1958) by* **RUTH MANNING-SANDERS**.

Lungile sat in the sunshine watching her mother put the finishing stitches in her isidwaba. It was a great occasion, for the isidwaba is the full skirt of black ox skins which no girl wears till her bridal morning. As it takes a long time to make, Lungile's father had prepared the skins many months ago. He had dyed them inkyblack with charcoal, till they looked quite like velvet. Then Lungile's mother shaped the skirt to fit tightly round Lungile's waist and fall into soft folds at her knee, and stitched all the pieces together most beautifully. Now the skirt was ready, and Lungile might set out for the home of her betrothed as soon as she pleased.

That evening she saw all the young women who were to accompany her to the wedding and arranged the day they were to leave. It was kept a deep secret; Lungile's mother and father would not expect to know, for every bride loves to slip away in the early morning without farewells.

Two days later, at the first flush of day, Lungile and her friends set out on their journey. It was early summer; the valleys and hills were covered with thousands of flowers, vivid scarlet or blue like the sky. The air was fresh and crystal clear, and the girls laughed and sang songs of travel. Lungile was full of joy, for her bridegroom was a chief's son, and she had chosen him out of many suitors. She was as cheerful and capable as she was lovely, and many young men had asked her to marry. She tilled the family's land, wove fine reed fences, and the beer she made was the best for miles around; there was no kraal where she would not have been welcome.

The girls journeyed together for some days, till at last they reached the bridegroom's land and went straight to his parents' kraal. His mother greeted them with every kindness, and showed them to a beautiful hut where they would stay till the day of the marriage. They had been expected for some time, and now every man and woman in the village was kept busy with the marriage preparations.

While the women ground corn or went out to gather wood, the bridegroom and his father considered what oxen should be killed for the feast.

"We will take two of those the Chief Maginde sent to me as your sister's marriage gift," said the father. "They are the finest in the herd, but my eldest son and his bride deserve the best."

The first ox was driven up and killed with much ceremony. When all was ready for cooking, and the guests already nearing the kraal, the meat was cut into long strips and set on the fire to roast. As the bridegroom's mother watched in horror, the meat began to jump about on the fire. It simply would not stay in place, and after trying to make it lie still twice, she became frightened.

"There must be witchcraft here!" said she, and hurried to call her husband to see this strange thing. She had left the strips of meat on the fire, but when she returned with all the family and guests at her heels, not a bit of the meat remained. All of it had disappeared.

"The animal was bewitched!" cried the father. Everyone looked at the bride's hut. She was a stranger and they suspected her.

"Bring the white bull," said the father. "He is the finest we have. Perhaps if we kill him it may break the spell."

The white bull was brought forward, the most splendid of all the cattle the bridegroom's father had received from Chief Maginde two years before. He was snow white from head to tail, save for two long black horns of great beauty.

The bull was killed and the meat cut up. This

time it was placed in large pots to boil. All stood by and watched; even the bride had heard of the trouble and waited anxiously in her hut, for witchcraft at her marriage was indeed a misfortune.

For a while all seemed quiet. Then the water began to boil in the pot in which the bull's head had been placed. Instantly there leaped out of the pot a fine young man, with a bearing like that of a great chief. He ran away with incredible speed, and even as he ran he changed into a handsome buck with large antlers. In a moment he was out of sight.

"Bring the bride here," said the Chief. "Without doubt, she is a witch and has brought trouble on us all."

A few minutes later, Lungile was brought from her hut with her maids.

"Go back home," shouted the Chief, "and never let us see your face again! You are not the wife for my son, nor would any decent family want you. I send you back to your parents and demand the return of my marriage gift of cattle."

"I am innocent of all harm," cried Lungile. "I have cast no spells and wish no evil to anyone."

"Go away! Go back to your village," shouted all the people there. "You have brought witchcraft here!"

Then they drove her out quickly; she did not

further attempt to prove her innocence but traveled home with her attendants in bitter anger.

Her father and mother were horrified when they heard of her treatment. They did not for a moment believe their daughter was a witch. The marriage gift was returned, and Lungile took her old place in the kraal again and worked as she had before. Only no more suitors came, for no one quite liked the story of the white ox with the black horns. It looked as if the skirt of black ox skins might never be worn.

More than a year went by, and Lungile gradually forgot her troubles. One day in autumn she went out to gather dried mealie stalks. The air was cool, the sun shone brightly over the great plains, and she sang gaily as she walked along the narrow path. Just as she was about to turn off toward the fields, a beautiful buck came in sight. To her surprise it did not run away but circled round her, running across the path and slipping in and out of the bushes. She thought she recognized him.

"Where have I seen this handsome animal before?" she said to herself and thought a minute. "Why it is the very same buck that jumped out of the pot at my marriage feast!"

For a moment she felt sad, then she threw back her head and laughed. "Now he will be caught. It is many days since we had meat. I will try to catch him as he passes."

The buck continued to dance around her, coming nearer and nearer, but always just slipping out of her reach. They had left the village lands behind and were drawing nearer to the mountains. She followed till they came to a stream which flowed down a green valley. There the buck stopped to drink, and Lungile jumped forward and seized him by the horns. He did not seem to mind and drew her with him on a path which ran up the valley near the stream. Lungile found the buck was far stronger than she expected. She could not turn him back, and she would not let him go.

The valley was empty and wild. High waving grass surrounded her. As they went on, a huge forest came into view which covered the lower slopes of a mountain. A blue shadow began to creep across the valley. Lungile saw it and thought, "I shall hardly reach home before dark. The buck is too strong for me; I must give him up."

She let him go with a sigh, and hurried back to reach the plains again before sundown. She had not gone far when she turned her head to see if the buck was still in sight. To her surprise he was following her. She stood still, and in a few minutes the buck was at her side.

"What do you want?" asked Lungile.

The buck only looked at her with his great brown eyes and said nothing. Lungile spoke again. She was sorry for the buck and felt sure that he was in trouble.

This time the buck answered in a soft, low voice, "Follow me to the forest yonder."

"I will come," said Lungile, and she turned once more to the great mountain and the forest at its foot.

 Before long they reached the first great trees, and there at the entrance to the forest they saw a sight which made Lungile cry out in terror. A huge ogre seated on a wolf was staring at them. Round his forehead he wore a string of animals' eyes which made him look even more horrible. Lungile turned to run, but the buck said to her calmly, "Come, and you will see what I can do," and he walked straight toward the ogre.

The girl followed but shivered as she heard the ogre say to the buck, "Ha! You will make a fine meal for the wolf, and that young girl will be my dinner!"

Then he stretched out his long arms and leaped forward to catch the buck. The buck did not move, but the instant the ogre's arms touched him, the buck changed into a powerful young man with a spear. The wolf ran off, frightened, into the bush. The ogre, taken by surprise, was slain with the spear.

The young man took the string of animals' eyes from the slain monster's head and threw them on the ground. Instantly they became living bucks. They all looked at the man with great affection and waited for his command.

The young man then turned to Lungile and said, "Will you be kind to these animals and help them? Remember I, too, was a buck."

Lungile nodded, and the young man went on. "Stay here for a few days and do this for me. Gather greens every morning at sunrise and chant this magic song." He sang:

> *Once my true love was a buck;*
> *Once my true love was a buck;*
> *Now he is changed to a strong young man.*
> *Now bucks, oh bucks,*
> *Change, change, and become young men.*

"I will do this," said Lungile with admiration in her eyes. "But tell me, are you the white ox who was killed at the marriage feast? And who are these bucks I will sing to?"

"I am that same white ox," said the young man.

"I am a great chief. Because my lands were better than Chief Maginde's and because I had finer cattle and stronger people, he hated me. One day he bewitched me and turned me into a white ox, and said that all my people should be deer. None should be free till I could change my form and become once more a man. He sent me as a marriage gift to the father of your betrothed—and so I came to be killed. You lost your first lover through me but do not grieve. You will be loved and honored if you will be my bride."

Lungile consented with great joy. She stayed at the edge of the forest for many days. Every morning at sunrise, she rose when the dew was still heavy, and sang the magic song as she gathered the green leaves up and down the hillside. And every day, more and more bucks came down from the mountains and clustered in the forest. They brought with them the does and the small fawns, and in seven days many thousand had gathered together. Then one morning as she sang the magic song, they all changed at the sunrise into men, women, and children.

This was how the enchanted buck regained his people and won a kind, courageous bride. Proudly, he returned with Lungile to her village. The marriage gift he gave to her parents was magnificent, and Lungile married the young chief amid much rejoicing.

This tale, retold by the editor, is from Fairy Tales from South Africa *(1908) by* **SARAH F. BOURHILL** *and* **BEATRICE L. DRAKE**.

MASTER-MAID

Once upon a time there was a king who had several sons. The youngest son grew restless at home and wanted to go out into the world to seek adventures. His father tried to dissuade him, but it was no use.

"Very well," said the king as he gave him his blessing. "You'll always find a welcome here when you return."

After the young prince had traveled for some days, he came to a giant's house and knocked on the door. The giant was very pleased to see him. He said he could certainly use the services of a young man who was strong and willing. So the prince was given dinner and a room over the stable.

The next morning the giant prepared to take his herd of goats out to pasture. Before he left he said, "You'll find me an easy master if you do as you're told. Today your task is to clean out the stable while I'm away. But you must not go into any of the rooms off the main hall or I will kill you."

So naturally, as soon as the giant went off with the goats, the prince became curious to see the forbidden rooms. The first two rooms contained large pots and various strange objects, but the third room contained a handsome, bright-eyed young woman.

"Well!" she said in surprise. "What are you doing here?"

"I've left my father's castle to seek adventure," said the prince, "and the giant has very kindly taken me into his service."

"You may regret it," said she.

" 'Tis easy work," said the prince cheerfully. "All I have to do today is clean out the stable."

"Yes, but how will you do it? For every shovelful of dung you toss out of the stable, ten more will appear. But I will tell you how to succeed. You must turn the shovel around and toss with the handle; then all the dung will fly out by itself."

"That sounds easy," said he. So he stretched himself out comfortably and talked all day with Maj (for that was her name) of this and that, and they became good friends.

In the later afternoon he went to the stable. First he tried using the shovel the usual way. The more he shoveled the faster the pile of dung grew. So he hastily reversed the shovel as he had been told, and the dung flew out the door. In a trice the stable was clean.

That evening the giant returned. "Have you cleaned out the stable?"

"Yes indeed, master."

When the giant saw the clean stable, he growled, "You must have been talking to Mastermaid."

"Mastermaid? What is that?" said the prince, pretending to look very stupid. "I did it myself the way we did it at home."

The next day before the giant set off again with his herd, he told the lad his task was to fetch home his horse from the hillside. Again he warned him not to enter any other rooms of the house.

As soon as the giant was gone the prince went to visit his friend Maj, the Mastermaid.

"An easy job today," he told her. "I've only to fetch his horse from the hillside. I fancy I can handle him no matter how fresh or skittery he may be."

"It's not as easy as you think," she warned. "Fire and flames will come out of the nostrils of the horse as soon as you near it. But I've discovered some of the giant's magic and I'll tell you what to do. Take the bit that hangs behind the door there and throw it right into the horse's mouth. Then he'll become tame."

So again the prince sat down to talk with Maj the

Mastermaid, and a very agreeable day they had. Maj told him she had been captured and kept prisoner by the giant but had been using her wits to learn some of the giant's magic spells. Giants, she said, were really not very clever.

"I'm not either," said the prince sadly.

"No matter," said Maj affectionately. "You have a warm heart and cheerful courage—that is what counts. You never seem to worry," she sighed. "I wish I could be so merry and lighthearted!"

"Aye, but it is your cleverness and wisdom that's saved me from the giant's vengeance!"

From this exchange you can guess that Maj and the prince were falling in love, and they spent the rest of the day talking of how happy they could be together if only they could escape the giant. The day passed so quickly that the prince had quite forgotten the horse until Maj reminded him of it when evening drew near.

Off he went with the magic bit, and, sure enough, the horse spewed out fiery flames as soon as the prince approached him. The prince threw the metal bit into the flames, and the horse became as quiet as a lamb. So the prince rode him home and waited for the giant.

When the giant saw the horse standing quietly in the stable, he roared, "You never did this task by yourself! You've been talking to Mastermaid!"

"Not me," said the prince, all innocence. "I'd like to see this Mastermaid you talk of."

On the third day before the giant went off with his herd, he said, "Today you must go to the devil and fetch me my fire tax." The prince whistled cheerfully as he went in to see Maj. He was confident that she would know how to deal with this task. "You must help me again," said he. "I've never been to the devil. I don't know the way nor how much to collect."

"Listen carefully and I will tell you," said Maj. "Go to the steep rock on the hillside, take the club lying there, and hit the rock three times. Out will come a creature glowing red, with sparks of fire darting from his eyes. Tell him your errand and when he asks how much gold, be sure to say, 'Only as much as I can carry.' If you do not say that, he will give you nothing."

The prince gave Maj a hug and said, "Och, without you I'd be mincemeat by now! But let's forget that and talk of other things." So he entertained Maj with light talk until soon she was laughing merrily and the day again passed quickly. Finally Maj warned him it was growing late, and it was time to collect the fire tax.

The prince climbed up the hillside to the rock and all happened as Maj had said. The fiery creature grumbled that the prince was lucky to know the right answer, but he gave him as much gold and silver as he could carry. He brought it back to the giant's house, singing gaily as he went.

"Where's my money from the devil?" demanded the giant as soon as he returned.

"It's there on the bench," said the prince.

"Now I'm sure you've been talking to Mastermaid," roared the giant. "I told you I'd wring your neck!"

"Mastermaid, indeed!" said the prince airily. "I wish I knew what it is. It must be a joke."

"You'll know tomorrow," snarled the giant.

The next day he took the prince into the Mastermaid's room and said to her, "Cut him up and boil him in that big pot for my dinner!" Then he went into the other room and fell asleep.

Taking all the old rags, shoes, and rubbish she could find, Maj put it into the large pot with water.

"Let the giant sup on that!" said she. Then she picked up a small sack of gold, a magic wand, a lump of salt, and a flask of water. From the shelf she took down a golden ball and a gold cock and hen. Tying them all in a large kerchief, she set off with the prince as fast as they could go.

In a few hours the giant woke up hungry and went to the pot for his dinner. As soon as he tasted it, he spat it out. When he found nothing but rags and rubbish in the pot, he knew what had happened. He let out an angry bellow that shook the house and rushed after them with long giant strides. It wasn't long before he saw them in the distance.

Maj threw down the lump of salt which immediately turned into a huge mountain. But that didn't stop the giant, who bored a tunnel right through the mountain.

Then Maj tossed out the water from the flask. The water became a broad sea, leaving the giant stranded on the other side.

Now they felt they were safe, so they set out at once for the prince's castle. But when they drew near, the prince insisted they must not walk up to the castle on foot like beggars. It was more seemly, he said, that Maj, his betrothed, should arrive in a coach. "Wait here but half an hour while I go home for the coach and horses in my father's stable. Then I can bring you properly to my father's castle."

Maj did not want him to do this. She had the power of foresight, and she knew further tests and danger lay ahead. The giant's revenge could follow them here. "Do not go back to the castle alone without me," she said. "Once you are there you will forget me and all that has happened between us."

"Don't worry, Maj," said the prince, "I could never forget you. I love you too dearly."

He was so eager to do her this honor that finally Maj assented. But she warned him, "You must go straight to the stables for the horses and return here. You must not speak to anyone. And above all, you must not eat anything. For if you do, we will suffer much grief and trouble."

The prince promised to do all this. He thought there was little chance he could forget his beloved Maj and their escape from the giant.

When the prince arrived at the king's castle, a great feast was being held, for his eldest brother had just been married. The castle was filled with a great crowd of people, and all were merrily rejoicing. The prince spoke to no one, nor would he eat anything. He went straight to the stables and harnessed the horses.

Now suddenly there appeared beside him a bewitching red-haired maiden who seemed to be one of the wedding guests, but she had, of course, been sent there by the giant.

"You must be hungry and thirsty after your journey," said she, smiling. "If you won't eat any food, at least have a bite of my apple."

 Hungry and thirsty he was—and bewitched as well—so he took a bite of the juicy apple. At once he forgot all about Maj. "I must be daft," he said. "Why am I harnessing a coach and horses?" He put them back in the stable and went along with the red-haired maiden to join the merrymaking.

The wedding celebration went on for weeks, as was the custom in those days. The prince was enchanted by the red-haired maiden, and at the end of this time, he was easily persuaded to announce their betrothal.

In the meantime Maj had waited for the prince's return. When he did not come back, she feared he was under a spell and had indeed forgotten her. But she had not saved him from so many dangers only to abandon him now. She knew a few spells herself!

So she walked on until she came to a deserted, broken-down hut. Here she decided to stay and at once set to work to clean it up. Then, remembering the giant's magic wand she had brought with her, she transformed the hut into a comfortable cottage with a garden of herbs and vegetables and a clutch of plump hens. Very quickly she became known around the countryside for her powers and skills.

The day for the wedding of the young prince to the red-haired maiden was set. But when the bride-to-be got into the coach, it broke down. The trace pin had broken; when it was repaired, it broke again. The wheel fell off; when it was replaced, it fell off again. No matter what was done, the coach could not be made to move. The bride sat inside raging with anger.

At the castle, the king was impatient at the delay. The guests, waiting for the coach to bring the bride, laughed at first to see it hopelessly stranded; then they grew uneasy. "The coach has a spell on it," they murmured.

The king's chamberlain, in charge of the procession, became more and more distraught. His wife, hearing the murmuring of the people, said to him, "Someone has cast a spell. There'll be no wedding unless you do something quickly. I've heard tell of a young woman at the edge of the forest who knows many charms. Send for her and she may be able to help you."

A messenger was dispatched at once. And thus it was that Maj was brought to the castle carrying a golden ball, a gold cock, and a gold hen. First she asked to see the prince who was to be married. Her request was granted.

Maj laid the gifts on the table before him. The gold hen pecked the golden ball over to the cock, and he with his beak returned it to her. Back and forth it rolled.

The prince was fascinated. "See how they share the ball, each with the other!"

"Yes," Maj replied, "just as you and I shared danger in escaping from the giant."

He looked at her in surprise for he did not recognize her. Then he picked up the golden ball. At once the giant's enchantment was broken. The prince exclaimed that he remembered everything, and they embraced each other happily.

The prince then told his father of his adventures, of his earlier betrothal to Maj, and how she had saved him. He said he loved her dearly and would marry no one but her, if she would still have him.

Maj said she would, for with her wisdom and his cheerful nature they were sure to live happily ever after. As for the red-haired maiden, she slid quickly out of the stranded coach and was never seen again in that country.

Variations of this Norse tale exist in Britain, Ireland, and Russia, places where the Norse settled over a thousand years ago. All the variations emphasize that the hero needs the heroine's wisdom in order to perform three very difficult tasks. **ANNE GOLID** *told this tale to Asbjørnsen and Moe, whose collection was translated by* **G.W. DASENT** *in* Popular Tales from the Norse *(1859).*

NOTES ON THE TALES

olktales are about human behavior in a world of magic and adventure. Underneath the entertainment of the surface story, there are usually one or more themes that illuminate the way the characters react, adding a deeper meaning to the tale. As noted in the preface, the tales teach moral and social values through the ways people deal with one another and the dilemmas that confront them.

Tales of Magic and Enchantment
In "The Enchanted Buck," the hero has been enchanted into an animal shape by supernatural forces of evil; he is doomed to exist in that shape until someone performs the specific rites which will break the enchantment and free him. The theme is of course familiar, but the heroine, Lungile, does

not sit in luxurious passivity until the spell is broken, as the heroine does in "Beauty and the Beast." She looks beyond the animal form to the spirit within and actively sets about aiding the hero to break the enchantment. While the specific ritual she performs is relatively easy, in terms of her culture it involves a great deal of courage and independence. Moving outside social and courtship customs, she accompanies a strange buck into alien territory, faces a monstrous ogre, and then is instrumental in freeing the young chief from enchantment.

Tales of Relationships

Several of the tales concern couples and the interaction of their behavior. The underlying themes emphasize the concept that mutual cooperation, as well as respect for each other's capabilities, are necessary to a couple's successful union.

The story of "Mastermaid" is in some respects "romantic," turning on the adventures of two young people in love—but on a deeper level, it comments on the positive way the two young people function as a couple. This is pointed out at the tale's end by the symbolic play of the golden hen and the cock with the ball, which signifies that only true partnership and cooperation can deal with the dangers of the world. Spells and enchantment are part of the plot, and it is the heroine, Maj, who enables the prince to escape the power of the giant. The young couple are more human and rounded in character than is usual in fairy tales—Maj, grave and serious; the prince, merry and impulsive. They are not a stereotyped fairy-tale couple, and the cheerful message here is that heroines may indeed have more wisdom and knowledge than heroes, and a hero need not be traditionally heroic nor excel in all things to be loved.

"The Lute Player" makes use of neither magic nor enchantment. It is the tale of a queen's wisdom and achievement, as well as an approving comment on flexibility in the relationship of a couple. The queen is left to rule in the king's absence. She then has to make a wise decision concerning the best way to ransom and rescue her husband. Rather than impoverish the kingdom and its subjects in order to raise the ransom, the queen resorts to her skill as a musician to attain her purposes. Because minstrels were welcomed in both castles and monasteries, their musical talents providing passport and "safe conduct," the queen disguises herself as a minstrel and uses the customary reward given minstrels as the means of her husband's rescue. In both this story and "The Legend of Knockmany" there is an implied equality in the conduct of the couple's affairs, and the wife's skills are essential in solving the couple's dilemma.

"The Legend of Knockmany" is a parody of earlier heroic legends, with a lively humor that makes for a good tale. There is warm affection between Oonagh and Fin M'Coul. Fin, for all his superhuman strength, relies on Oonagh's imagination and practical wisdom to get him out of a tight corner. Her strategy succeeds brilliantly; the problem of Cucullin is disposed of permanently; and Oonagh ends up with her long-desired rearrangements in house and property.

"The Shepherd of Myddvai and the Lake Maiden" occurs in a number of variants in Wales; all of them attribute a family's medicinal lore to the wisdom of an earlier pagan deity, a local lake maiden or goddess. The mating of a local divinity with a mortal is an ancient theme. While in Greek myths such unions often had unfortunate results, in this tale of the Celtic lake maiden, the outcome is a blessing. The lake maiden settles quite easily into ordinary rural folk life and bestows the usual gifts of fertile crops and livestock. But she does state her own terms for the marriage, and the mortal husband keeps to their agreement. Their years together are contented ones. The brief glimpses we are given of the couple show the same mutual concern and respect found in the other tales of happy and successful unions.

Tales of Family and Community

Many of the tales deal with what could be called "family bonds" and, to some extent, a sense of community.

"The Search for the Magic Lake" is a South American tale told by Inca Indians. Although the story is primarily about young Súmac's quest for magical water to cure an ailing prince, the warmth and strength of family bonds are clearly stressed. The success of the quest brings an offer of "adoption" by the royal family and the higher status that that implies. Súmac refuses the offer in order to return to her family; further, all that she asks is that her reward benefit her brothers and parents.

Heroines in the folktales of pre-revolutionary China deferred to traditional family and social codes. In the tale "The Young Head of the Family," the heroine uses her wisdom and cleverness to achieve a position of power within that structure. Her abilities are recognized. Still, the rewards of her achievement are for the benefit of her family.

Tales of Wit and Humor

Cleverness is a valued quality in many folktales, and

it appears in varied forms. In "The Young Head of the Family," the cleverness or wit of the heroine is shown in both her quickness with riddles and her shrewdness with financial matters.

Norse tales often display an earthy humor and the peasant's irreverence for authority. The Norwegian farm lass in "The Squire's Bride" is both independent and clever. She refuses to be coerced into marriage and easily eludes the clumsy trap set for her. With a broad sense of humor, she repays the pompous squire in his own coin, as he finds himself before the minister with a bay mare arrayed in bridal clothes.

In "Kamala and the Seven Thieves," the hardworking, resourceful Kamala not only makes the wasteland thrive, but cleverly preserves her earnings from the plotting of a band of thieves. There is sharp humor in Kamala's strategy, akin to the imaginative cleverness of Irish Oonagh and of the Norwegian farm lass.

Tales of Old Women

One of the tales in this collection portrays a cheerful, capable old woman. Endowed with practical wisdom and a sense of humor, the merry old woman in "Bucca Dhu and Bucca Gwidden" is staunchly unafraid of supernatural creatures. The theme here is her right to live her own life in her own way. She refuses to conform to her son's staid, conventional ideas of what an old woman should be. Her individuality not only makes for an engaging tale, but also suggests to children that old people have the right to be themselves and enjoy life on their own terms.

Tales of Independent Women

In "Kupti and Imani," the two sisters are opposites. Kupti is passive and submissive—but later displays malicious jealousy. Imani is active, demanding of life the freedom to make her own choices. Poverty does not daunt her; she uses her skills and imagination, plus hard work, to build a serene and contented life and eventually makes her own choice in marriage. The moral appears to be that submissiveness can lead to frustration and malice, while independence and rewarding work bring satisfaction and contentment.

All the tales in this collection were chosen for their positive themes, as well as for their resourceful heroines. Bringing the underlying themes of these tales into sharper focus can give the adult reader a clearer insight into "messages" that are sometimes overlooked; the attitudes and values implicit in these stories from centuries past remain just as pertinent to our modern times.

SUGGESTED READING

Gaiman, Neil. 2015. *The Sleeper and the Spindle*. New York: HarperCollins.

Goble, Paul. 1993. *The Girl Who Loved Wild Horses*. New York: Aladdin.

Hamilton, Virginia. 1995. *Her Stories: African American Folktales, Fairy Tales, and True Tales*. New York: Blue Sky Press.

Lansky, Bruce. 2002. *The Best of Girls to the Rescue: Girls Save the Day*. Minnetonka, MN: Meadowbrook Press.

Martin, Rafe, and David Shannon. 1998. *The Rough-Face Girl*. New York: PaperStar Books.

McGoon, Greg. 2015. *The Royal Heart*. Lakewood, CA: Avid Readers Publishing Group.

Ragan, Kathleen. 2000. *Fearless Girls, Wise Women, and Beloved Sisters: Heroines in Folktales from around the World*. New York: W. W. Norton & Company.

Sand, George. 2014. *What Flowers Say: And Other Stories*. Translated by Holly Erskine Hirko. New York: The Feminist Press.

Yolen, Jane. 1986. *Favorite Folktales from around the World*. New York: Pantheon.

———. 2000. *Not One Damsel in Distress: World Folktales for Strong Girls*. Boston: Houghton Mifflin Harcourt.

ACKNOWLEDGMENTS

My sincere thanks to local librarians, too numerous to name, in the Nassau County Library System and to librarians in the Donnell Children's Branch (New York Public Library) for their help and enthusiastic interest in my project. I also want to express my appreciation for the guidance and unfailing support given by my editors at the Feminist Press, Corrine B. Lucido and Sue Davidson.

Grateful acknowledgment is made for permission to reprint the following copyrighted material:

Barlow, Genevieve, "The Search for the Magic Lake," from *Latin American Tales* by Genevieve Barlow; copyright © 1966 by Rand McNally and Company; reprinted by permission of Genevieve Barlow.

"The Stars in the Sky," from *More English Fairy Tales* (1904). McNally and Company; reprinted by permission of Genevieve Barlow.

Manning-Sanders, Ruth, "Bucca Dhu and Bucca Gwidden," from *Peter and the Piskies* by Ruth Manning-Sanders; copyright © 1958 by Ruth Manning-Sanders; reprinted by permission of Harold Ober Associates, Inc.

ETHEL JOHNSTON PHELPS *(1914–1984) held a master's degree in medieval literature; she was coeditor of a Ricardian journal and published articles on fifteenth-century subjects. Originally from Long Island, her activities included acting, writing, and directing in radio drama and community theater. Three of her one-act plays have been produced.*

SUKI BOYNTON *is the senior graphic designer at the Feminist Press. She is a graduate of Connecticut College with a BA in art history and has a degree in graphic design from the Art Institute of Charleston, South Carolina. She currently lives in New Jersey.*

The Feminist Press is a nonprofit educational organization founded to amplify feminist voices. FP publishes classic and new writing from around the world, creates cutting-edge programs, and elevates silenced and marginalized voices in order to support personal transformation and social justice for all people.

See our complete list of books at
feministpress.org